"Jordan, *_____*
Nick said.

She turned away. "Good-bye, Nick. It's been . . . interesting."

"Is that what you call this?" he asked, his voice rough. He buried his fingers in her hair, using it as an anchor to allow him easy access to her parted lips. His mouth was a weapon of warm, searing heat, conquering hers with a kiss that demanded her surrender.

"Stop, Nick. I can't play this game." Jordan moaned.

"Oh, lady." He sighed. "This is no game."

Some treacherous corner of her heart wanted to believe him. But she knew that now, or later, he'd leave her. "Nick, I don't want you to kiss me."

"You don't?" he asked between kisses. "If I really believed that, no matter how much I wanted you, I'd stop, Jordan. But I don't believe you. Look me in the eye and tell me you don't like it when I kiss you."

"I don't!" she answered, still weak from his kisses and aching for more.

"Liar."

She started to argue, but his mouth swooped down on hers in a quieting kiss. Jordan felt as if every nerve in her body had been transported to her lips. She was aware of nothing but the feel of his mouth on hers.

"That's what you're going to get whenever you try to lie to me," Nick promised. "Admit it, you feel the fire between us, but you're afraid you'll get burned. . . ."

WHAT ARE *LOVESWEPT* ROMANCES?

They are stories of true romance and touching emotion. We believe those two very important ingredients are constants in our highly sensual and very believable stories in the *LOVESWEPT* line. Our goal is to give you, the reader, stories of consistently high quality that may sometimes make you laugh, sometimes make you cry, but are always fresh and creative and contain many delightful surprises within their pages.

Most romance fans read an enormous number of books. Those they truly love, they keep. Others may be traded with friends and soon forgotten. We hope that each *LOVESWEPT* romance will be a treasure—a "keeper." We will always try to publish

LOVE STORIES YOU'LL NEVER FORGET
BY AUTHORS YOU'LL ALWAYS REMEMBER

The Editors

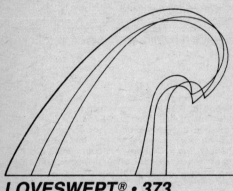

LOVESWEPT® • 373

Joyce Anglin
Feeling the Flame

 BANTAM BOOKS
NEW YORK • TORONTO • LONDON • SYDNEY • AUCKLAND

FEELING THE FLAME

A Bantam Book / January 1990

LOVESWEPT® *and the wave device are registered trademarks of Bantam Books, a division of Bantam Doubleday Dell Publishing Group, Inc. Registered in U.S. Patent and Trademark Office and elsewhere.*

If you would be interested in receiving protective vinyl covers for your Loveswept books, please write to this address for information:

Loveswept
Bantam Books
P.O. Box 985
Hicksville, NY 11802

ISBN 0-553-44009-8

Published simultaneously in the United States and Canada

Bantam Books are published by Bantam Books, a division of Bantam Doubleday Dell Publishing Group, Inc. Its trademark, consisting of the words "Bantam Books" and the portrayal of a rooster, is Registered in U.S. Patent and Trademark Office and in other countries. Marca Registrada. Bantam Books, 666 Fifth Avenue, New York, New York 10103.

PRINTED IN THE UNITED STATES OF AMERICA

O   0 9 8 7 6 5 4 3 2 1

One

The notebook was just out of her grasp, nestled near the center of the cockpit. Jordan Donner stretched hard, leaning into the Jet-Ranger, lifting one foot off the pavement and straining to reach the light blue binder. A bead of perspiration trickled between her breasts, and she swore under her breath. Why did she have to wear such a tight skirt in the first place? she groused silently. Publicity and their dumb ideas! How was she supposed to do a convincing promo when she couldn't even climb into the helicopter without hiking her skirt up to her waist?

She puffed a strand of auburn hair out of her eyes and reached further, balancing on the ball of her foot and angling her body for extra length. Closer . . . closer . . . Her fingers touched the tip of the spiral. "Gotcha, you pesky little—"

"Hey! Get out of there!"

Behind her, the voice boomed like a thunderclap. Jordan jumped, whipping her head toward the sound, too frightened to scream. She hadn't seen anyone when she'd crossed the helipad of KJTX-TV, not even a security guard. Weakly, she slumped half in, half out of the Jet-Ranger and inhaled a ragged breath of dry Arizona air.

"What do you think you're doing, lady?"

She stared at a chest, all she could see of the speaker from her precarious position. Her stomach fluttered, and she swallowed a dry lump. *At least he could apologize for scaring her,* was her first thought. Her second was that he had a very nice chest. And that she'd dropped her notebook again.

"Hold on a minute," she said, a little too breathily. She cleared her throat and tried again. "I'll be right with you."

"Get out of the helicopter, please. Now."

"Just a sec," she muttered, groping for her book.

"Time's up." His low warning came just as his hands closed around her waist, lifting and pulling.

She had a fleeting sensation of solid strength. "Wait!" Indignation clashed with embarrassed heat when her bottom brushed against what was—definitely—the lower half of his anatomy. Forgetting the spiral, she squirmed out of his grasp. "How dare you!" she demanded, catching a glimpse of a rock-hard chin as she struggled to her feet. "How dare—"

Before she had completely gained her footing, he grabbed her wrist and, with a slight tug, yanked her away from the helicopter.

"Whaaa . . . what are you doing?" She tried to pull her arm free. "Let go of me!"

The man's only response was to tighten his grip.

"Stop it!" Her voice rose, matching her growing panic. "You can't do this!"

"The hell I can't, lady. I gave you fair warning." Without even a glance in her direction, he stepped up his pace, pulling her behind him like a recalcitrant child.

"Let go!" She clawed at his hand with embarrassed fury. "If you don't let go right now, I'll—" Before she could threaten him with the station's security guards, the man stopped short, whirling to grab her by her upper arms. His abrupt movement brought her within a hairbreadth of his body, and her hands shot up, splaying against his muscular chest. Her head snapped back, and her gaze locked with a pair of bedroom eyes as black as a moonless night. The man's features were taut, ruthlessly handsome even in his apparent anger, and oddly . . . familiar?

"What do you want?" she demanded, ignoring the slight flutter in her stomach as she glared up at his rugged face.

"Right now, I want you to stop that infernal screeching."

His gaze lowered to her mouth, and his hold changed subtly, but Jordan scarcely noticed. *Screeching?* She never screeched! And what if she had? She was entitled. This stranger was manhandling her. Irate, she shoved away from him. She felt a solid thunk and heard a low hissing of air before she found herself standing free, staring at the dark-eyed stranger in stunned disbelief. She'd elbowed him but good!

He clutched his side. A muscle ticked in his jaw. She tried to feel sorry she'd hurt him, but after all, she hadn't intended to do him any harm, while his actions had been so . . . *crazy.*

A slow dread inched up her spine. Was it possible he was some sort of mental case? she wondered. This was a news station. What if he had some grudge against KJTX? What if—?

The man stepped toward her again, and Jordan backed away, letting her active imagination run rampant. She remembered the steel of his grip. Crazy people were supposed to be uncommonly strong, weren't they?

Stay calm, she ordered herself, trying to remember everything she'd ever heard about dealing with the mentally ill. Talk softly, stay calm. She offered a weak smile.

"I didn't mean to hurt you." She watched his eyes for any sign that he was about to attack again. "But you can't go around just . . . just grabbing people like that."

He stared at her, pinning her with his dark gaze. His angular features appeared carved out of granite. The only softness to his face was his mouth; if the full, cleanly etched curve could be called soft. Jordan's own mouth went dry while she waited for his response, trying to plan what her next move should be. But he just watched her, as inscrutable as a still-life photo.

Another discomfiting wave of recognition swept over her, but she shrugged it aside. If she had ever seen him before, it was probably on the wall of the Phoenix Post Office.

Still trying to smile, she plotted her next move. He stood between her and the station, yet the helicopter offered little protection. Which way to go?

"I wouldn't try it, if I were you." His words were slow and deliberate. "I'll only have to stop you again, and this time I won't worry so much about being gentle."

"Gentle!" She clutched her probably bruised elbow.

"If you'd done as I asked in the first place, your arm wouldn't be sore. And neither would my ribs. Who'd have thought such a skinny little—" His eyes narrowed and perused her like a slow, hot wind. "No, definitely not skinny."

When his gaze lingered on her breasts, she felt an uncomfortable stirring. Her mind reeled at the purely feminine reaction; it had been a long time since she'd . . . since a man had . . . But not *that* long.

She looked away, fighting the distracting train of her thoughts. Where was the damn security guard? she wondered frantically. If she moved too fast, would the stranger try to grab her again?

As she moved tentatively, he took a step toward her.

"Don't come near me," she ordered, inclining her head toward the building behind him. "Take one more step and I'll scream. Loud enough to bring out every man in that station."

"Don't be silly," he warned. "If you did something like that, I'd hand you over to security. And then you'd really be in a mess."

"*Me!* You attack me, and think I'll be in a mess?"

Nicholas Estevis raked a hand through his hair and tried to figure out if the gorgeous little trespasser was bluffing. Why did the ditzy ones always have to be the best looking? he wondered. And why did this one have to make him feel as if he'd never seen a real woman before? He didn't want any trouble. He just wanted to check out the station and then get the hell back to Estco.

A slight movement drew his attention back to her, and he walked his gaze over her delicious figure, experiencing the same jolting rush as when he'd first seen her. Her breasts were full and firm, her waist femininely small. He remembered how her bottom had felt snuggled up to his groin. He also remembered the fiery sparks in her haughty glare and the lush curve of her hot-tempered mouth. He felt some of his irritation subside. He didn't want any trouble. What he wanted to do with this particular trespasser had nothing to do with trouble. It would be pleasure. Pure pleasure.

"I did not attack you," he stated. "I merely—"

"Yes, you did!" Jordan nearly stamped her foot in fury. "You sneaked up behind me and grabbed me! You hauled me halfway across the helipad. God only knows what might have happened if I hadn't escaped from you."

"You're not even close to escaping." He spoke as if she were dull-witted. "And if I'd been attacking you for what you've got in mind, I sure wouldn't do it in a"—he grimaced—"a parking lot.

"Furthermore, if I ever did 'attack' you, as you so charmingly put it, it would be with your whole-hearted cooperation." The corners of his mouth twitched. "Sort of a mutual attack."

Jordan's mouth dropped open, but no words would come. Who was this man? And why did he look so familiar? She couldn't remember ever dealing with anyone quite so self-deluded, and she'd dealt with a lot of swelled male egos in her twenty-eight years.

"Should I take your newfound silence as agreement?" he asked. Though his tone held no trace of humor, she was sure his eyes were dancing.

Jordan wondered if his grin had anything to do with the fact that her eyes were about to pop out of their sockets.

"Why you . . . you . . . you must be totally out of your mind!" she insisted. She found his grin just a little too engaging. "No wonder you have to resort to attacking defenseless women."

"You? Defenseless? No way. And I did not attack you."

He moved closer with each word, but this time Jordan felt no fear. She was struck again with that feeling of awareness; as if something was hovering in the shadows of her memory.

"I was only protecting private property," he said. "Namely, that helicopter."

"That's ridiculous," she said. Then she remembered the security guard. She eyed the stranger closely, taking in the cut of his trousers, obviously custom-tailored to fit his muscular legs and trim waist. And no ready-made shirt would fit his broad shoulders with such perfection. He wore his rich apparel with the careless elegance of one used to having only the best. And though she was thoroughly familiar with the trait, she hadn't realized it could be so provocative. No, she concluded, he was no security guard.

"See anything you like?"

Jordan looked up to meet his laughing gaze, and in one mortifying instant realized she'd been staring. At his body. "What I'd like," she blurted, watching him watch her in a way that made her pulse race, "is to know who you are and why you grabbed me like that."

"I told you. I was protecting my helicopter."

His helicopter. Something in Jordan's mind

made a tiny click, but she couldn't put a finger on it. No longer certain of her ground, she tried a new tactic. "That helicopter belongs to KJTX."

If smiles could strut, his positively swaggered. "And KJTX belongs to me."

She gulped. She knew Estco, a large corporation based in Phoenix, had purchased KJTX a month ago. Steven Estevis, the new acting station manager, had hired her three weeks after the acquisition.

Suddenly the tiny click locked in. Lord, where had her mind been? She'd read about the man behind the corporation many times. According to all the papers, one successful venture after another put him in the business world's spotlight. Though only thirty-three, he'd carved a huge niche for himself in the world of high finance. And only a little less frequently, his photo appeared in the shadowy pictures of the society columns. He was almost as famous for his romantic escapades as he was for his business deals.

Jordan's shoulders sagged as she admitted to herself that the man standing before her had to be the absentee owner, the man who had every female at KJTX abuzz.

"Nicholas Estevis," she said with a resigned sigh.

"Now that we know who I am, that brings us back to you." A dark brow lifted expectantly.

She squirmed. Go ahead, Jordan, her mind jeered. Tell Mr. Estevis you work for him. Tell him his new reporter didn't recognize the face that's been in every paper in the Southwest. Her attention to current events would impress him.

"Don't worry," he said, when she didn't answer. "You won't be in any trouble." A smile as smooth as silk slid across his face. "In fact, I'd be happy to give you a personal tour of the station someday. But the helicopter is strictly off-limits. Why don't you leave your name with the receptionist and I'll call you later in the week."

She stared at him in wide-eyed amazement. *Call her?* Nicholas Estevis thought she wanted him to call her? Hah! The day she became interested in such a womanizing egotist was the day she'd voluntarily commit herself.

"You do have a name, don't you?"

His tone sent rivers of defiance rushing through her. Lord, how she hated the condescending attitude that usually accompanied wealth and power. She thought she'd seen the last of that when she'd divorced Clark and moved to Phoenix. Well, Nicholas "Casanova" Estevis could save his sexy smile and come-hither eyes for someone who was interested.

"Mr. Estevis," she said firmly, "you have the wrong impression. I don't want a tour of the station. I don't need one. I—"

"Hey, Jordan!" a familiar voice interrupted.

She turned her head. Clayton Mathers, senior pilot/reporter for KJTX, was walking toward them.

A smothered oath brought Jordan's attention back to Nicholas, and she was surprised to see him studying her with narrowed eyes. He watched her for a moment, then leveled his gaze at her colleague.

Clayton approached with his usual rolling gait. The boyish grin that had won the hearts of many female viewers spread across his craggy face. She could almost see the wheels spinning beneath his shaggy blond hair; turning in quite the wrong direction, she was sure.

"Nick! Well, hi there, buddy," Clayton drawled, his West Texas accent more prominent than usual. "Didn't know you were back."

"I flew in early this morning." Nick shook Clayton's extended hand. "I couldn't leave things to run on their own while Steven is in New Orleans."

Jordan was a little surprised by the warmth in Nick's voice after the look he'd originally shot at Clayton. But the smiles covering both men's faces attested to genuinely friendly feelings.

"Sure good to see you, ol' buddy." Clayton hesitated slightly before adding, "Didn't mean to interrupt anything."

"You didn't interrupt a thing." Jordan said hastily. "Mr. Estevis and I just met. In fact, I haven't even had a chance to introduce myself yet."

"Well, well." The playful humor in Clayton's blue eyes was obvious. "I always knew you were a fast mover, Nick, but don't you think you should wait until you at least know the lady's name?"

"We were just getting around to that."

Clayton chuckled. "Looked like a pretty involved introduction to me."

"No, nothing involved." Nick looked briefly at Jordan. "Yet."

Jordan understood his implication, and, judging by the knowing look that passed between the men, so did Clayton.

"Now just a minute, you two!" She felt like shaking her fist in both their faces. How dare they act as if the outcome of this bizarre meeting was a foregone conclusion?

"First of all," she fired at Clayton, "Mr. Estevis and I weren't involved in anything except an absurd misunderstanding. He thought I was a heli-

copter groupie or something. And as for you—"
She turned her attention to Nick, and was momentarily robbed of speech by his mocking smile.

"Yes, Jordan?" he said.

His smug tone sent her temper over the edge.
Well, she'd soon wipe that look off his face.

She raised one hand and toyed with the second
button of his shirt as she said, her voice deliberately honeyed, "You're my boss, big boy."

She stepped away and watched his expression
change.

"I'm Jordan Donner," she announced, dropping
all the cloying sweetness from her voice. "And I'm
the new pilot/reporter for KJTX."

Satisfied with his stunned look, she turned on
her heel.

"What the—You come back here, Jordan!" Nick's
heated commands and Clayton's laughter followed
her as she made a fast exit for the station.

"By the way, Clayton." Jordan threw the words
over her shoulder. "Could you get my notebook
for me? I didn't have a chance." She blew a quick
kiss in Nick's direction. "*Nicky* kept me much too
busy."

Two

As Jordan stepped out of the July sun's glare into the fluorescent corridor of KJTX-TV, the air-conditioning blasted her like an arctic front. She whisked down the hall, her mind whirling to the staccato clicks of her heels.

Big boy! She'd actually called him "big boy." Would she ever stop letting impulse overwhelm reason? She remembered her father's favorite words, "You're overreacting again, Jordan." She was mortified, but in this particular instance, her father was right.

Her eyes blinded by the sun's glare, she didn't notice a shadowy silhouette step directly into her path until it was too late. The impact as she smacked into the figure coming toward her knocked her off balance and her hand swung out, fingers grasping for support. She caught an arm, sending the papers that had been tucked in the crook of that arm fluttering in all directions.

"My files! Oh, heavens! My files!"

Jordan recognized Cora Scott's voice just as the executive secretary's face came into sharp focus.

"Are you all right?"

"Just look at this mess!" Cora's angry nod almost disrupted the lacquered perfection of her hair.

Jordan dropped to her knees and scrambled along the hall, gathering the drifting papers. "I'm really sorry, Cora. The sun—" She faltered. No explanations would soothe Cora. She turned to gather more sheets and came face-to-face with a knee. A masculine knee, encased in navy blue slacks. She closed her eyes and dropped her head. Maybe she should have just stayed in bed all day.

"Another attack, Ms. Donner?"

Jordan opened her eyes and lifted her gaze to a stubborn chin and mocking smile.

"Just a small accident."

"Doesn't seem to be your day, does it?"

That, she thought, was a masterpiece of understatement.

"Here, let me help." Nicholas picked up a paper just out of her reach.

"Oh, no, Mr. Estevis!" A girlish gush came from behind them. "I'll take care of it."

Jordan turned, astonished. Cora was whisking up papers with the energy of a whirlwind. A perky smile replaced her customary frown, and Jordan would have bet that Cora's thickly mascaraed lashes were batting at least ninety beats per second.

Disgusted by the coquettish fluttering, Jordan gathered the last of the papers, then shifted her weight awkwardly. A tanned hand extended toward her. Nicholas was crouched beside her, a confident smile etched on his rugged face. His gaze flitted to her skirt, and she realized what he must already know: She couldn't possibly get to her feet without assistance. Her skirt was too narrow, and her heels just high enough to make rising with any dignity embarrassingly tricky.

With a resigned sigh, she placed her hand in his outstretched palm. His fingers closed over hers, creating a medley of impressions: the warmth of his touch, the power of his grasp, the texture of skin against skin. Never had the subtle differences between a man's hand and her own been so vivid to her. She glanced at him as he helped her to her feet, and, strangely, saw no trace of mockery.

"I'll take my papers now," Cora said, breaking the silence.

"Here you are, Cora," Nicholas said. Detaining Jordan with one hand, he used his other to pass the pages.

"Cora," Jordan said, "would you like some help getting the files back in order?" *Say yes. Please say yes.* Funny things were happening to her metabolism, and the catalyst seemed to be Nick's hand. The longer he held hers, the warmer she got. And when she tried to pull free, the slight tightening of his hold warned of an imminent tug-of-war.

"No, thank you, dear," Cora simpered.

Nick's mouth twisted into a smug grin. "If you're sure you can manage on your own, I have a few matters I'd like to take up with Miss Donner."

"Oh, but I need *you*, sir," Cora said. "Right away."

Jordan felt a sudden fondness for the woman.

"I've been looking everywhere for you," Cora continued. "You need to sign for a delivery that just came."

Nick's smile wavered.

"The messenger refuses to accept any signature but yours."

His grasp loosened, and Jordan pulled her hand free.

"Damn," he swore.

Jordan took the opportunity to ease down the hall, her hand still tingling from his touch. She had to regain her composure. Jordan Donner did not get weak-kneed over playboys.

"I know what it is," he said. "I'll take care of it right away."

"Oh, and I put several calls on your desk that need to be returned right away. And these are the papers you wanted to review before your meeting with Mr. Bancroft. I'll have them in order by the time you're finished with your calls."

As Cora's voice droned on, Nick's posture stiffened. Jordan knew he wanted her to stay put. And for the briefest of moments, she was tempted. *He* tempted her, she admitted. She liked the way he looked. She liked the way she felt when he touched her. But he was her boss, she reminded herself. And she wasn't going to confuse physical responses with emotional ones. Not ever again.

When Jordan joined him on the helipad, Clayton was cleaning the cockpit windshield, his sunglasses pushed low on his nose. As soon as he saw her, he shoved them back in place and smiled broadly.

"Nick catch up with ya?"

"Sort of." Jordan reached into her pocket and retrieved her own sunglasses, took a clean rag from the pile near Clayton's feet, and wiped at an imaginary spot.

"You shouldn't be doing that in your fancy duds," he warned. "Wouldn't want you to get all grubby."

"It can't be helped. I forgot to bring a change of clothes."

"You mean you overslept again and didn't have time to double back and get them."

She bit her lip, aggravated that he'd come to know her so well in only a few days. "As I said, it can't be helped."

"Sure it can. I'll handle the mechanics until your flight suits are ready."

A trickle of perspiration worked its way down her back, and Jordan squinted into the azure sky. The Jet-Ranger received a thorough going-over, including the engine, twice a day. It needed to be done now, before the metal surface became too hot.

"It doesn't matter." She shrugged. "Mark cornered me a little while ago, and we got the publicity shots in the can. I'm free to get as grubby as necessary."

Clayton's easy laughter drifted over her like a cooling breeze. "Must be those green eyes of yours. It always takes him at least an hour to get a good shot of me. Says my pictures look like I don't have any eyeballs."

They lapsed into companionable silence, but Jordan knew from the way his head kept darting in her direction that Clay was dying of curiosity. And it wasn't about her photo session.

"So?" He finally asked.

"So?"

"So what'd you think of Nick?"

"Oh, well, it's too soon to tell, but I suppose he'll be like any other boss. The only time we'll hear from him is when he doesn't like something or wants to change some—"

"Nice try, Jordan."

She glanced up. Clay was still wiping the windshield. And he was grinning again. "What?"

"You know darn well I don't mean the *businessman*. I mean the man. What do you think?"

She sighed, then stalled, but he wouldn't give up.

"Okay! For Pete's sake." What *did* she think of Nick? "He's very attractive, he's rich. Successful," she decided aloud. "Every woman's dream."

Clayton stopped wiping. "How come you make that sound more like a complaint than a compliment?" He turned his attention back to the windshield, spraying the cleaning solution on the glass and watching it dry almost before he could blot it with his rag.

But he didn't fool her. She knew he'd listen carefully to her answer.

"Men like Nick live in a different world from most people. They have their own morals, their own codes." She shook her head. "I don't know. I guess I just don't understand all the rules."

"What makes you so sure there are any?"

"I was brought up in that world. And I never fit in. My father took great pains to remind me that a man of his stature expected certain things of his family. And my ex-husband took equal pains to remind me how miserably I'd fail—" She stopped short, embarrassed by her disclosure.

"And you've decided Nick must be just like them?"

She covered her discomfort with a show of indifference. "It doesn't really matter what I think. He's my boss. That's all. I don't have to like him. Just work for him."

Clayton stopped cleaning and watched her from behind the dark brown lenses. "Most women like him."

"That's because all they see is the flashing white teeth and beach-boy body."

"Noticed that, did ya?"

"I'm only human."

He pulled off his glasses, his blue eyes showing an uncomfortable understanding. "Get to know the man behind that face and body," he advised. "You might be surprised at what's there."

"Sure, Clayton." She knew she'd do no such thing.

"Good." He smiled. "But give him a chance to get used to being around here for a while first. He's a mite testy about having to fill in while Steven's in New Orleans." He shot her a speculative look and chuckled. "But then again, he might just decide it's not such a bad deal after all."

Sunlight streamed through the window in her small office, lending it a sense of tranquillity amid chaos. Jordan still got a little thrill every time she walked into the space she shared with Clayton. It marked another step, another advance in the course she'd plotted for herself. Soon, she'd be there. Independent, successful. So much more than just a rich man's daughter and a playboy's ex.

Her desk was covered with notes written in her almost perfect script. A piece of pale blue paper taped to the telephone caught her attention.

With a sinking feeling in the pit of her stomach, she knew intuitively that the note was from Nicholas Estevis. She picked it up and tried to decipher all the abbreviated scratches. It figured that he'd write with bold disregard for the art of penmanship. When Jordan had decoded the message, the sinking feeling in her stomach turned into a gigantic hole.

She'd been summoned to his office. At eleven o'clock. Sharp. He'd underlined "sharp" as if she might otherwise show up at five before twelve. And then he'd added the stinger. He'd signed it "Your Boss," a cutting reminder of her earlier behavior.

For the rest of the morning, each passing moment seemed an eternity. When it was finally eleven, she didn't need to check her appearance. She knew from the fifteen previous checks that her blue silk blouse was neatly tucked beneath the waistband of her summer white skirt and that her shoulder-length hair looked as good as possible after being ravaged repeatedly by her nervous fingers.

Cora was waiting for her in the executive suites, a professional smile on her too-red lips.

"Mr. Estevis told me to keep an eye out for you," she said in her best executive-secretary voice. "He assumed you'd think his office was here, but for some reason he's taken that little cubicle down by the lunchroom."

Jordan murmured her thanks and turned to leave.

"Yes, dear. You'd better hurry." The red lips stretched wider. "You wouldn't want to be late. Again."

Jordan cringed. If Cora knew she'd been late this morning, so did a lot of other people. Including Nicholas Estevis. Was that why he wanted to see her? But she knew she was grasping at straws. Nicholas was interested in a whole lot more than her time. She could read it in his eyes. She could handle that. What really worried her was what he'd been able to read in hers.

When she reached his office, she paused to collect herself before knocking. Though the door was closed, she could see him through a viewing glass set in the heavy oak entrance. He was leaning forward in his chair, head bent over a file folder. Sunlight illuminated the healthy glow of his thick raven-black hair. She noticed that only the ends curled, giving him a tousled look, as if he'd just left a lover.

She closed her eyes. She couldn't allow her imagination to run rampant. She was certain that if she walked into the office with anything even remotely romantic in her head, he'd pick up on it like a metal detector spotting buried treasure.

Sensing her presence, Nick watched Jordan hover outside the door. He'd love to replace the pristine collar of her blouse with his hands and move slowly down to . . . He brought himself up short in a rush of frustrated anger. He had a reason for calling this meeting, and it wasn't to entertain idle fantasies. He motioned for her to enter, then he consciously tried to push back his annoyance. His irritation had been building since he had opened her personnel file.

At first, he'd been certain that Jordan Donner's presence at KJTX was staged, one of Steven's off-the-wall attempts to "loosen up big brother." Why else would a so-called pilot/reporter be dressed like a fashion plate instead of wearing a regulation flight suit? Why else would she accuse him of attacking her one minute, bat those long lashes at him the next, and top it all off by playing cat and mouse in the hall? It would be just like Steven to orchestrate some elaborate practical joke.

But when he'd found Jordan's personnel file, he'd realized this was no prank. Her credentials, sketchy though they were, were real. He'd even called Whirly Girls to verify that Jordan Donner was indeed a member of that prestigious organization of women helicopter pilots. And then he'd begun to get angry. Steven should have consulted him before hiring such a novice. Even though KJTX was under his brother's control, Steven knew damn well Nick expected to be consulted on any decisions.

"Well, Ms. Donner," he said, irritated when Jordan continued to hesitate near the door. "Are you planning to come in sometime today?"

She stiffened, then regally crossed the room to a chair he pushed out for her. When she crossed her knees, her skirt rode up her leg, giving him a tantalizing peek at her shapely thigh.

"You wanted to see me?" she asked coolly, jerking her skirt down.

"Yes, I did." He lowered himself to his chair and steepled his hands beneath his chin, fighting an amused grin. "Thank you for not disappointing me."

Her face pinked, and the fire he found so intriguing sparked in her eyes. "What is it you wanted to see me about?" she asked stiffly.

"Several things. I'm very curious about you, as you can well imagine."

"I'd be happy to discuss any questions you have about my employment, Mr. Estevis."

Was it her tone or the situation that ignited his temper again? He didn't really want to discuss her job. He didn't want any part of KJTX, no matter how lucrative the venture might prove to be. Damn Steven for insisting Estco buy the station. And damn him for not being more conscientious when he'd all but threatened to quit if he wasn't given complete control over his pet project.

Nick raked a hand through his hair and sighed with frustration. He hated having to come in behind Steven and clean up, but there was no point beating around the bush. "As far as I'm concerned, Ms. Donner, you may not *have* a job here after today."

"What?"

Her face paled, and Nick felt a twinge of regret, but he couldn't back down. "I've been going over your personnel file." He picked up a folder. "You have no previous experience as a flight reporter. No previous experience in journalism. No background in television. In short"—he dropped the folder back on his desk—"you have no qualifications for this job other than the fact that you're a licensed helicopter pilot. And for that, you don't have enough flight hours under your belt to ensure competence, much less expertise."

"Wha . . . what?" Her body went rigid with shock. "Steven said, I mean—I don't understand."

"I thought it was obvious." Nick rocked back in his chair and peered at her through narrowed eyes. He didn't like the feeling that flooded him when she said his brother's name with such easy familiarity. And he didn't like not liking it. "I'm trying to understand Steven's reasoning in hiring you."

"But I thought you knew!"

"I knew nothing about you until this morning. Managing this station was to be a trial run for my brother, and Steven had no right to jeopardize you, or the integrity of this station, by hiring someone with so little experience."

She leaned forward and met his gaze head-on. "Whether you like it or not, he *did* hire me. And I have a contract with KJTX. You can't fire me."

His temper got the better of him. "I'm aware of your contract, Ms. Donner. What I want to know is how you convinced Steven to give it to you!"

"Convinced!" Her voice rose a notch. "You make it sound as if I forced him into it!"

"I wasn't thinking in terms of force." He voiced the idea he found so disturbing. "Something more like . . . gentle persuasion."

"Are you insinuating that your brother and I . . . that I . . . that there's something more between us than business?"

Sparks flew from her eyes. Her back stiffened. Nick had the feeling she would gladly reach across the desk and knock his block off, if she could. He knew in that instant he'd been way off base to think she'd used Steven to get the job. He was wrong. And he was absurdly relieved.

She closed her eyes and took several deep breaths. Without conscious thought, Nick moved from behind his desk to offer the apology she deserved. He waited until her breathing slowed down, then rested his hand on the back of her chair and leaned as close as he dared.

Jordan felt Nick's presence even through the red haze of her anger. She opened her eyes and looked directly into his velvet-black irises.

"Am I forgiven?" he asked softly, holding her gaze with the power of his. A wry hint of humor danced behind his solemn expression. "I didn't realize you had such a temper, Jordan. May I call you Jordan?"

For a moment, his tentative smile of truce lulled her, but only for a moment.

"Most women tend to get rather angry when insulted, Mr. Estevis."

Nicholas settled himself on the corner of his desk, stretching his long legs in front of him with confident grace.

"I apologize again, Jordan. Clearly I was mistaken."

"I'm glad you recognize the absurdity of your insinuation."

He threw back his head and laughed, white teeth flashing. "Oh, Jordan! One look at your face and I knew there was no way in hell you were involved with Steven. A woman might look embarrassed at being found out, or a little flustered, but no woman would be able to look that furious if she'd been sleeping with an Estevis."

Jordan didn't know whether to laugh or scream. It was obviously another ego trip for him to think the name Estevis, when linked to the bedroom, was synonymous with a trip to heaven.

"Well?"

"Well what?" Jordan made her voice enigmatic, though she knew perfectly well what he was asking.

A slow grin spread across his handsome face.

"You're not going to give me a break, are you?"

"Not until I think you deserve one."

"Okay. I'll accept that." The sculpted planes of his face lifted and softened as his smile became more entreating. "Will you accept my apology?"

"Possibly." She hedged, remembering back to the times she'd forgiven too easily because of a winning smile, a coaxing plea. "Am I to assume you no longer have any objection to my employment?"

His posture stiffened. "Not for a minute." He reached across the desk and picked up her file. "Nothing in here has changed." He flipped through the pages. "You still aren't qualified. And I can't risk your safety or the station's image because Steven is impulsive. He should have consulted me before making his decision. It might have saved us all some embarrassment."

"I'm not embarrassed. And I doubt very seriously Steven has any regrets about his decision. There are some things about me that aren't in that file, Mr. Estevis. Some very important things."

"Such as?" he demanded.

"Such as the fact that though I didn't get a degree, I minored in journalism in college."

"That would help," he conceded. "But knowing some journalism and being a good reporter don't necessarily go hand in hand."

"And all the flying hours in the world won't make you a competent pilot if you don't have good instincts, and good hands. I can do this job, Mr. Estevis. I can help this station. And that's the bottom line, isn't it? Building the ratings."

"That's our initial goal."

"Well, KOOL proved several years ago, when they

were the first to hire one, that a female pilot/
reporter can build ratings. If she hadn't been killed
on that search-and-rescue out in Colorado, there's
no telling how far—"

Both of them jumped at the shrill clang of the
telephone.

"Excuse me for a second." Nick turned, reaching for the phone.

Jordan allowed his movement to take her mind
from the topic of their conversation. Her gaze
followed the clean line of his torso. There wasn't
an unnecessary ounce of flesh hidden beneath
the clinging white shirt, she was certain of it. Her
stomach clutched in a response that was becom-
ing annoyingly familiar.

She listened to his confident tone as he spoke.
His voice played over her senses like soft, slow
music. She watched his mouth, the sensual shape
of his lips as they parted to form words or smiles
or tilt down in an arrogant frown. She wondered
what it would feel like to kiss him, to feel her lips
parting under the pressure of his and . . .

Her heart began to pound, wrenching her mind
from the dangerous direction of her imaginings.
She couldn't afford to think like that. Not even for
a minute. She didn't want an involvement—even
an imaginary one—with her boss. Or her boss's
boss. Later, after she'd proven herself, well, maybe
then she'd find a man who'd really appreciate all
she had to offer.

She pulled a wall of reserve around her, fighting
off an unexpected pang of longing when she looked
at Nick. He raised a hand and signaled he was
winding down the conversation. When he finished,
he replaced the receiver and glanced at his watch.

"I'm sorry," he said, though the gleam in his eye looked like anything but regret. "We'll have to continue this discussion later. I'll pick you up about seven."

"What?"

"Seven," he repeated with maddening self-confidence. "I'll pick you up for dinner at seven."

"Dinner?" she repeated, feeling as if her brain had gone on hold.

"Tonight. Dinner. You. Me. I thought it was pretty self-explanatory."

"Are you crazy?" she blurted before she could stop herself. "First you attack me, then you threaten to fire me, then you insult me, and now you expect me to have dinner with you?" She tried to keep her voice calm. Surely he must see the absurdity of his suggestion.

The look he shot her was a cross between exasperation and amusement.

"I should have known better than to think you'd make this easy." He shook his head. "One thing is clear, Jordan. You definitely know how to keep a man on his toes."

"I'm not interested in keeping you on your toes, Mr. Estevis. I—"

"Nick," he interrupted. "Or Nicholas, or"—he winked—"Nicky."

"Mr. Estevis!"

"Nick." This time there was a light threat to his tone.

"Oh, all right! Nick!"

"Good." He gave her a smile she would bet had sent the hearts of better women than she crashing to his feet. Hers was fluttering in traitorous excitement, reminding her she was sadly susceptible to his charm.

She sagged. "I know I'm going to hate myself for asking, but considering everything, how can you sit there and invite me to dinner as calmly as if nothing had happened?"

"Because nothing *has* happened?"

She ran her fingers through her hair and tried to figure out if she was missing something. Had she imagined all the innuendos he'd fired at her throughout the morning? Was she the only one who felt the tension whenever they looked at each other.

"Jordan." His voice was soft, low, silky.

She looked up, not knowing what to expect, and nearly drowned in his fathomless gaze. She became lost in the warm black velvet; she wanted to pull the warmth around her like a blanket and rest in the quiet of the dark.

"Jordan." He did not break the hold of his gaze. "I want you to have dinner with me tonight."

"I don't think that's a good idea."

He pushed himself off the desk and took her hand.

"We don't have time to argue about it," he said, drawing her to her feet. "I have a meeting scheduled in twenty-five minutes, and it's at least a thirty-minute drive from here. Say yes, Jordan."

Her mouth moved to form the word no.

"You have to have dinner with me so I'll know you accept my apology. You never did say you forgive me. Besides, actions speak louder than words."

Again her mouth formed the word no, and again he interrupted. "It's business, Jordan. I'll pick you up at seven."

"No," she finally said, meaning to stop there.

She couldn't possibly go out to dinner with him. "I'll meet you there."

Had those words come from her mouth?

Nicholas smiled, really smiled. "Fine," he said, ushering her out the door. "Seven o'clock. Simon House."

Then he was gone. Before she could catch her breath, he was down the hall and out of sight. She sagged into the wall and placed her forehead against the cool surface.

What had she got herself into now? she wondered again as she tried to sort out exactly where she'd gone wrong. What, oh what, had she done?

But the current of excitement shooting through her each time she visualized his face, remembered the warmth of his touch, told her exactly what she'd done.

She'd made a monumental mistake.

Three

Nick's attention was only half on Estco's projected profit margin for the next fiscal year, but half his attention was all it ever took with such reports. What bothered him was where his mind kept wandering, his body in hot pursuit. It made him uncomfortable, and not just physically.

Oh, he'd wanted before. But it had been an uncomplicated wanting, demanding only an agreeable and agreeing partner. Now that wanting had a name, a face, a personality.

There was something in Jordan Donner's eyes, an intenseness, a wary bravado, that mesmerized him. Beneath her sleek exterior was something that didn't fit. Something that touched him. Maybe it was only his sense of curiosity or some misguided sense of protection. Whatever it was, it made him uncomfortable. But it didn't stop him from wanting her; wanting to explore her with his hands and his mouth, to touch her and hold her, to see her eyes burning with passion.

He shifted in his chair, leaning forward as if he were really interested in what Dave was saying instead of merely trying to hide his arousal.

"—looks good, Nick."

"What? What does?" He felt himself blush for the first time in years.

"The figures, Nick." The accountant shot him an indulgent look. "I knew we should have postponed this meeting until you'd had a chance to rest."

"Nonsense. I'm fine."

"So what is it? Hearing how rich you're getting bores you?"

Nick had the grace to feel chastised. "Sorry, Dave. I know you went to a lot of trouble to—"

"Now who's talking nonsense? You keep all your books in such tight order, I don't know why you even keep me on." David Bancroft crossed the sitting area of his office to take a chair directly across from Nick. "No, forget that." He looked around the plushly appointed area. "I need your fees to keep me in the style to which I've become accustomed."

Nick laughed. "Me and about two hundred other clients."

"Most of them hired me after you took me on. I owe you a lot, Nick. You've been like a brother to me ever since Bill died. I don't want you to overwork yourself."

Nick's heart thudded, as it did each time Bill's memory stirred. His gaze skimmed the surface of Dave's desk, flickering over the silver-framed picture of his best friend. He couldn't bring himself to study the smiling, relaxed face. After all these years, he still couldn't look at Bill's picture without remembering, without experiencing those feelings of helplessness he so despised.

"Take a vacation," Dave encouraged. "You're entitled, you know."

"Maybe I will." He caught Dave's doubting look. "As soon as Steven gets back."

Moss-green eyes and a soft, tempting mouth filled his mind, erasing the hard, ugly memories. Yeah. Maybe he would take a vacation. Smack-dab in the middle of Jordan Donner's bed.

Jordan paused in the entry of the restored turn-of-the-century house, waiting for her nerves to settle. She fingered the lace of her cream-colored Victorian-style dress and noticed, to her absolute horror, that her fingers had started to tremble.

She was being absurd. This was a simple business dinner, for Pete's sake! Nick wasn't going to drag her down to the floor and ravish her under the table.

The image of cool, dark Nicholas Estevis doing something that outrageous was so ludicrous that her nervousness began to evaporate. She checked the time, noting it was almost seven, and approached the reservation desk.

"Ah, yes, Ms. Donner," the hostess, a slight woman with a sprinkling of gray in her brown hair, said. "Welcome to Simon House." She stepped from behind the reservation desk and gave a discreet signal to a nearby waiter.

"George, will you please escort Ms. Donner to Mr. Estevis's table?" Her voice hinted the request was more of a privilege than a task. "Mr. Estevis will be joining her momentarily. Nick's always very prompt," she told Jordan privately.

And very popular with a certain hostess, Jordan thought, as she accompanied the waiter to an intimate table for two in an alcove at the far end of the dining area. All around the restaurant were thick green ferns hanging from the ceiling and palms set in brass pots serving as natural dividers, giving each table a sense of privacy. But there was so much greenery around hers, it seemed almost isolated.

In order to fight her nervousness, she tried to concentrate on the view outside the bay window. Behind the lace curtains, lush patio gardens with colored lights beckoned. In the center of a flagstone patio, a fountain trickled daintily. Jordan imagined how the scene would have looked a century ago, with willowy ladies, skirts draped over rounded bustles, strolling along the gas-lighted path from the patio to a gazebo at the far end of the yard.

She sat admiring the view, lost in a world of gentler times, when she felt a tingling sensation run up her spine. She didn't need to look to know that Nicholas was approaching.

Oh, great, she thought, now *she* was developing radar. She turned her head, hoping she was mistaken and the tingling had been caused by a draft.

It hadn't been. Nick stood near the edge of the alcove, a smile lighting his bronzed features. He wore a tailored jacket that accentuated his broad shoulders, and matching slacks. She smiled weakly.

"Hello, pretty lady," he said, as he crossed the small space separating them.

"Hello, Nick." She was aware his name rolled easily and naturally from her tongue. She looked away, not wanting to feel familiar with him. But his dark visage filled her senses again, proving she had no control over where her mind chose to wander.

"You look lovely tonight, Jordan." His rich baritone was as warm as a Phoenix night.

She glanced up. "So do you."

She cringed.

He laughed.

"You must have just arrived," he said as he seated himself. "The men in the dining room are still slack-jawed from watching you walk through. You look like a vision out of the past." His voice softened. "Too beautiful to be real."

Her eyebrows arched in pleased surprise. Surely this wasn't the same Nicholas Estevis who'd made mincemeat out of her self-confidence this morning?

"Thank you," she murmured, waiting for the other shoe to drop. Such a flowery compliment would probably be followed by a disclaimer.

But none came. Jordan raised her eyes to his and found he was looking at her with genuine appreciation. His gaze held none of the amused speculation or outright sexual desire evident in their earlier meetings, but simply the open appreciation of a man for a woman. She suddenly felt beautiful.

The waiter appeared, and after settling on her order, Jordan used the few moments while Nick selected a wine to savor his compliment. She wrapped it around her like a blanket and warmed herself in the glow it left. It was ridiculous, she knew, to get such pleasure from so little. And she was going to put it out of her mind. She really was. As soon as she finished wallowing in it.

She felt his gaze on her and was suddenly self-conscious. She scoured her mind for something to say—anything to break the mounting tension.

"Warm, isn't it?" she heard herself asking, and wished she could slide under the table and disappear.

"Getting hotter by the minute." A devilish gleam lit his eyes.

· A smile worked its way across her face. He was such a charming scoundrel. Instead of making her more uncomfortable, his light flirting put her at ease.

"Shall we share all our deep, dark, secrets?"

"I don't have any," Jordan answered in a tone calculated to match the lightness of his. "I'm just a plain old working girl."

"Most working girls I know don't have a license to pilot a helicopter, much less have an entire ad campaign built around their face."

She blinked in surprise and relief. If Nicholas knew about that, he must have heard it from his brother. "Steven told you?"

"Actually, I figured it out for myself. I know my brother pretty well, and I knew there was a logical reason for hiring you. When I added that to the way you were dressed today, it all worked out to advertising."

"Have you talked with Steven today?"

"Briefly. I caught him just as he was leaving the hotel. He didn't have time to go into detail, he just said he'd purposely kept you a secret from me." He bared his teeth in what could have been a smile. "Sort of a welcome-back surprise. Steven's always been a real kidder."

Before she could answer, the waiter appeared

with a wine bottle. Nicholas tasted it, nodded his approval, and the waiter filled Jordan's glass. She sipped the dry white wine, savoring its taste, reflecting on Nick's discreet sampling. Clark had always made a show out of approving the selection; smelling, swirling, tasting, with an exaggerated display of each step. Nick hadn't tried to impress; and that *was* impressive.

Then she noticed him watching her over the rim of his glass, his dark eyes glowing. She took another sip and felt his gaze follow the course of her wine, the intensity of his look deepening as it moved slowly down her throat, and lower.

Her nerves prickled with awareness. "This is the first time I've actually been glad I'm not on call-out yet," she said, setting the wineglass back on the table.

To her great relief, Nick's gaze rose to meet hers. He lifted an eyebrow questioningly.

"I wouldn't be able to drink if I were on call. And this is delicious."

"I know that a pilot can't have any alcohol in his system," Nick said. "But what's this about not being on call—yet?"

"Clayton and Steven are waiting until I find an apartment closer to the station before they put me on call-out. You know," she added, seeing his frown, "the time factor. Right now I live over thirty minutes from the station."

Nick leaned forward in his chair. He seemed on the verge of an explosion. "Are you telling me that you're moving closer to the station so you can be on call? At any and all hours of the night? That Steven actually agreed to that?"

Though his voice was carefully controlled, Jordan didn't mistake the anger beneath each word. His irritation confused her.

"Of course I'll be going on call-outs. Didn't you discuss all this with Steven?"

"No!" he snapped. "We reviewed his idea to hire a female in order to get a larger ratings share. We agreed your looks would be a natural draw. We did not discuss call-outs in the middle of the night, or flying under pressure during hazardous conditions without enough rest, or sapping what strength you have by working long, grueling hours." A muscle ticked in his jaw. His voice was strained. "Have you both lost your minds?"

She glared at him. "Have you? Surely you knew that even if I was hired for PR reasons, I would still have to perform the job in its entirety? Why, if I didn't, I'd be doing nothing more than fluff pieces and public appearances!"

"Exactly."

"But that doesn't make any sense! The main reason KJTX needs another reporter is to give Clayton some time off. Being on call twenty-four hours a day, seven days a week, is too much for anyone, male or female."

She could tell by the set of his jaw she wasn't convincing him. His anger made her uneasy, but she plunged on.

"Why are you so dead set against me? All I want is to do a good job for you. You seemed perfectly content when you thought I was going to do nothing more than fly around and look pretty."

"Have you ever seen a dead body, Jordan?"

Her eyes widened at the unexpected question.

"Have you ever seen bodies burned beyond recognition?"

Her stomach turned at the image.

His eyes were cold. "How are you going to handle it the first time you're called out and you find a light plane down in the desert, a whole family wiped out?" His gaze searched her face, waiting for her to betray the horror she'd feel.

"I'll . . . I'll handle it the same way Clayton does. I'll cover it."

"What will you do if something goes wrong with the chopper?"

"I know emergency procedures. I'll handle that too."

Nick sighed and looked away, pulling on a mask of cool control. Lord, she was stubborn.

"Jordan, flight reporting isn't just a job." He captured her gaze again. "It's a way of life. It takes—"

"I know what it takes," she interrupted. "That's one of the reasons I want it so badly. I'm not just looking for a *job* until Mr. Right comes along. I want this chance. I'm a gifted pilot. I have intelligence and compassion and drive. I have so much to give, so much I want to accomplish. I wa—"

She bit off her words as the waiter reappeared, serving dishes of beautifully arranged chicken paella with almonds and mushrooms. Despite the delicious aroma of the mingled spices, Jordan knew she wouldn't be able to touch a bite until she had things straightened out. Toying absently with her salad fork, embarrassed over her outburst, she wondered what to do next.

"Let's forget about this for tonight," Nick said, reaching over to stroke her fingers with a touch as gentle and soothing as his voice. "After all, I agreed to give Steven complete control over KJTX.

I couldn't fire you, *or* give you a raise, even if I wanted to. Let's just relax and get to know each other."

"That's not going to help a thing." She pulled her hand free. He was trying to manipulate her. Well, he could forget it. She was going to carve her own niche in this world. She was going to prove her worth. And she would never, ever again let any man dictate what she could or couldn't do.

"It might help if we get to know each other," Nick repeated. "I make it a practice to spend some time with my key employees. I like to know what to expect from them, what their goals are, and how far I can trust them."

"You can expect my best and trust me to give it. I'm a good pilot."

"But inexperienced." His dark eyes seared her. "You have less than a thousand hours."

"Steven thought it was enough."

"Steven didn't watch his best friend, a man with over three thousand hours, fly his helicopter into a stand of trees. Steven didn't have to help his family cope with their grief. Steven didn't—" He broke off, masking the emotions behind his words with a look of stony resolve.

"I'm sorry." Jordan's heart twisted. She knew the words were inadequate.

"No." His tone was emotionless. *"I'm* sorry. I shouldn't have brought it up, but I want you to understand something. This is the first time Steven has ever been given unlimited authority. KJTX is his project. I have to make sure he hasn't made a mistake in hiring you. I don't know how he'd react if this venture turned into a fiasco."

He picked up his fork and speared a piece of

chicken. "Now, can we forget about business for a while?"

"I thought business was the reason for this dinner."

"That's the reason you accepted." His eyes gleamed wickedly. "But that's not the entire reason I asked."

She watched his lips as he spoke, registering the sensuality of his full bottom lip, the slightly pouty look it had when it wasn't stretched into an arrogant smile. Her pulse began to race in spite of herself.

"Oh, of course," she said, forcing her attention away from his mouth. "The apology."

He hesitated. "Not exactly." But before she responded, he changed the subject.

"What did you do before you went to work for Bell?"

"You know about that?"

"It was in your personnel file. Sixteen months at Bell in Dallas. Almost a year at Brown's Transport Service. College three years before that. What came in between?"

She steeled herself. "I was married," she said reluctantly. She didn't want to talk about those years, but decided she should. When she explained to Nick that her ex-husband had been in televison; that she'd spent hours at the studio where his syndicated talk show was taped, Nick would understand she had some experience. Oh, sure, she hadn't any formal training, but she'd picked up quite a bit of working knowledge.

Nick masked his surprise. "Is he the one who got you interested in helicopters?"

"Inadvertently," she admitted. "I needed something to fill my time while Clark was working."

"Did he approve of the way you *filled* your time?"

She sighed. Nothing she'd done had ever won Clark's approval. "He didn't care one way or the other—"

"How long have you been divorced?" Nick interrupted, staring at her.

"A little over two ye—"

"Do you stay in contact with him?"

"Of course not. We have nothing—"

"Then you're not still carrying a torch?"

Her temper started perking. "No! I am not carrying a torch!" She glared at him. "Didn't anyone ever tell you it's rude to interrupt?"

His mouth turned up into a smile, and he chuckled. "Repeatedly. I'm afraid I frequently don't do justice to my mother's strict upbringing. She was forever mourning that all her hard work to raise me as a gentleman went for naught."

As he spoke of his mother, his eyes sparkled, and Jordan could almost feel the love behind each word. That was a facet of his personality she'd never suspected: the doting son. Listening to Nick made her long for something she'd never known. Love without qualification. Was there such a thing? she wondered. She played with the idea for a few moments, then tucked the dream away.

Nick watched Jordan intently, intrigued by her transparent emotions as he spoke of his family. Interest, delight, longing. So open, so fascinating. And then, like a doe caught in an open meadow, she'd shy away at the mention of her own memories. But he wanted to see behind her wall of reserve. He had an unreasonable need to knock down her defenses and touch the woman within. He wanted to know if her passion matched her fire, if her heart matched her spirit. And he wanted to know if her skin was as soft as it looked, if her mouth tasted as sweet as he imagined.

"So?" Jordan said as she finished the last bite of her dinner. "What do you do when you're not working?"

"Nothing special. Swim a little. Dive."

"Scuba?"

"No. Springboard. Platform. I stopped diving competitively years ago, but I still enjoy it." He grinned. "It helps me stay in shape."

It certainly does, she mused, conjuring up an image of him in bathing trunks.

"What about you, Jordan?"

"Oh, I read some. Go hiking in the mountains with a couple of friends. Fly whenever I get—"

"Friends?"

"You're doing it again!" she said with a reproving glance.

He smiled broadly. That smile had probably saved him from his mother's wrath on many occasions, Jordan thought, feeling her own irritation melt.

Her heart warmed as she looked at him, a soft smile touching her lips. His wit, his charm, fascinated her. Suddenly the atmosphere changed. She met his gaze and felt the tension spark between them.

"I thought about you today." His voice enveloped her like a fine mist, sending chills down her spine. "In fact, I couldn't stop thinking about you." His gaze slid over her, turning her chills to shivers. "Did you think about me?"

"Nn-n-o." She knew he could tell she was lying.

It would be so wonderful to get away with one little fib. She'd always been such a terrible liar. She often wondered if her nose grew or her ears twitched.

Nick lifted a sleek brow, a gleam of amusement sparking the midnight tinder of his eyes. He reached across the table to toy with her fingers. She felt the warm, solid strength of the man within his touch.

"Tell me the truth, Jordan," he demanded in a soft, husky voice. "Did you imagine how it could be between us? How you would feel in my arms?"

Her heart began to pound, and she tried to ease her hand away, but his fingers tangled with hers and held her prisoner. She wanted to get angry. Red-hot, blistering angry. She wanted to tell him how arrogant, how conceited he was. But she couldn't muster anything worse than mild indignation.

"No," she answered, grateful he hadn't said anything about swimsuits. "Such insanity never crossed my mind."

He laughed, a deep, happy laugh. He squeezed her fingers lightly, then rubbed his thumb across her knuckles in a strangely erotic motion. Jordan's pulse started racing again, but this time she couldn't blame it on indignation.

"I like you, Jordan," he said, surprising her. "I never know what to expect from you."

She had to agree with that. Even she didn't know what she was going to do or say when she was around him. He kept her so off balance she had a difficult time merely concentrating on what was happening, much less on how she was going to respond to it. All she knew for certain was that she felt excitement at his touch, pleasure in his company, and that warning bells were going off in her head.

She was dangerously close to forgetting who he was, the kind of life he lived. She'd had enough of the fast, high living he exemplified. That kind of lifestyle had contributed to her mother's early death, and been a major point in the failure of her marriage. Clark had never understood why she couldn't conform to the wild social set's mores, or rather, the lack of them.

She tried to regroup by attacking. "I suppose most of your women friends fall all over you after a line like that?" She hated herself for the flicker of jealousy when she thought of Nicholas flirting with other women.

"That wasn't a line, Jordan. I wanted you to tell me you've been thinking about the same things that have been driving me crazy all day."

He sounded so sincere she was almost ready to believe him. Almost.

"Why should I spend my time thinking about something that's never going to happen?"

"How can you know it's not going to happen?" His eyes took on a rakish gleam. "Unless you've already considered it."

"I haven't!"

"Then how do you know?"

"Because I'm thinking about it right now!" she blurted, flustered.

Her skin grew hot as she really did think about it: a fantasy of Nick lowering his mouth to hers. She could see his eyes closing as his face drew nearer, feel his breath tease her lips just before his mouth covered hers in a long, exploring kiss. It was so real that her lips tingled and her eyelids grew heavy.

"Christ, Jordan. Don't look like that or I'm going to take you up on your offer and kiss you—right here, right now."

"What offer? What are you talking about?" She tried to sound confused and felt her nose growing again.

"You just don't give an inch, do you?" Though his voice held a hint of laughter, his eyes were boring into hers, seeking out the darkest recesses of her soul. "Why are you so afraid of what's happening between us?"

Cold panic gripped her. It was time to stop this. A little teasing might be all right if it were between two other people. But it wasn't possible between them. Not for her. The warm persuasion of his touch was too powerful, the tender probing of his gaze too tempting. It had been so long since she'd dared let anyone get this close. She had to make him understand that she couldn't play this kind of game. She didn't know all the rules. And even if she had known the rules, something told her that Nick didn't always play by them. She took a deep breath, preparing to tell him he was going to have to look elsewhere for amusement.

"Don't say anything yet," Nick cautioned before she could get her thoughts organized.

She looked up in surprise, wondering if he'd somehow divined what she was going to say.

"You know, Jordan, you have a very expressive face."

He leaned his elbow on the table and studied her. Hooking his thumb under his chin, he absently stroked the full curve of his mouth. Back and forth, up and around. She tried to look away, but she couldn't drag her gaze from the hypnotic movement. His fingers looked so strong. His mouth so firm, yet soft. Sensuous. She couldn't focus her mind on anything else.

His finger stopped moving. His mouth formed words she scarcely heard. But she did hear. And the words brought her out of her sensual daze.

"I don't believe you're really a coward," he stated calmly. "The woman I met this morning gave every bit as good as she got." He smiled wryly. "Maybe even a little better. So why does this have you in such a dither?"

"I'm not interested in having an affair." Had she really said that? She tried not to think how brazen she sounded.

"What are you interested in?" His tone gave no hint as to whether he'd even understood that she'd taken it for granted he wanted to have an affair with her. "Talk to me, Jordan."

"I'm interested in my career," she said curtly. "In making a life for myself."

"And what about people? What about friends and family? Where do they fit in? What about love?"

"Don't you mean lovers? Isn't that what all this is about?"

"No. It's about you. I want to get to know you, as a woman. I want to know what makes you the way you are. How your mind works. What you feel."

She searched his expression for some sign of deceit, but he sat unwavering under her scrutiny. Could she have misread him? she wondered. Was she so used to being glossed over as just another pretty face, just another warm body, that she'd failed to recognize genuine interest?

"My father is in Los Angeles," she answered slowly, deciding to take a chance that Nick was being honest. "We're not very close. My mother died about ten years ago. Since I moved here, I've made a couple of friends. Good friends," she added, thinking of how much she'd come to rely on her relationship with Todd and Gary. She was safe with them. They weren't interested in her, or any other woman, as more than a friend. She accepted them and they accepted her. No games, no demands.

"What about old friends? Surely you had some close friends when you were growing up."

He had unwittingly plunged into another danger zone.

"I think we're getting off the subject," she said. Her tone was sharper than she'd meant it to be, and she wasn't surprised when his eyes narrowed.

"Okay, Jordan. Let's get back on the subject. Why are you fighting something that's as strong and as inevitable as the need to breathe?"

Her temper soared.

"Inevitable? You think that just because two people are attracted to one another falling into bed is inevitable!"

"Now hold on a minute. I'm not talking about bed-hopping, and you know it!"

"Oh? Then should I take this as a proposal?"

He paused and raked his hand through his hair, though his gaze never lost its hold on her. She could see the iron determination in his eyes, the inner struggle to master his temper. When he spoke, his voice was low and controlled.

"I've already tried marriage. The only proposals I'm making these days are business ones. What

I'm talking about isn't marriage or bed-hopping or one-night stands or whatever else your active imagination can conjure up. I'm talking about attraction. Plain and simple. It's there, Jordan. Every time our eyes meet, every time we touch. The fire is there, and no matter how hard you try, you can't deny it."

Jordan didn't want to hear what he was saying, didn't want to know he could read her so well. She didn't want to feel her blood pounding and her heart racing. She didn't want to acknowledge that he excited her, made her feel things, want things, she'd convinced herself didn't exist for her anymore. She didn't want to. But he was right. She did want, she did feel.

"All right, Nick. I'll admit there's an attraction. But I learned a long time ago not to play with fire." She paused long enough to assure herself that he knew she was serious. "And that's the end of it."

She picked up her purse and scooted back her chair, preparing to leave.

"You can't just leave it like this," he said, tensing as she rose.

She looked down at his perplexed face and felt some of her anger melt. At least he'd been honest with her. He hadn't tried to camouflage his desire with words of love. He probably never needed to. She was sure women were his for the taking. He'd just picked the wrong one this time.

"I can leave it like this," she told him softly, a dull ache starting in her heart. "There's nothing else I can do."

Jordan didn't look back. She could feel his eyes on her, knew he was watching her wend her way through the crowded dining room. The chills down her spine were the only proof she needed. She quickened her pace, wanting to get out the door and out of his line of vision, to forget that for just a moment she'd actually been tempted to stay.

Nick dropped the telephone receiver back in its cradle after the sixth unanswered ring and glanced worriedly around his office. Where was Jordan? She should have been home by now. Had something happened? No, no, he wouldn't think that. But he shouldn't have let her leave the restaurant without him. He should have followed his instincts and gone after her. Then he could have made sure she arrived home safely, and he wouldn't be in the office trying to call her right now.

He glanced at his watch. He'd give her another five minutes before he called again. If she didn't answer that time . . . He forced his hand away from the phone. Five minutes. He could wait that long to hear her voice. And he *would* hear her voice. She was all right.

Restlessly, he flipped through her personnel file again. A reluctant smile worked across his face when he glanced over her credentials. Lord, she was something. So little experience, such limited background; and yet, enough determination to stand toe-to-toe with him and fight for herself. He liked that. Nick frowned. He just wished she'd use that same strength when dealing with him on a personal level. She was a good match for him. Why couldn't she see that?

Impatient, he glanced at his watch again. Two more minutes. If she'd just let him pick her up and take her home, he wouldn't be sitting here, sweating out a couple of minutes. To hell with it. He was going to call. As he punched out her telephone number, he visualized the best route from Simon House to her apartment. One ring. Two. If she didn't answer this time, he was going to . . .

"Hello?"

Her voice sounded strange, and he could hear background noises, like something heavy hitting the floor. Anxiety struck him like a blow. "Jordan. Are you all right? Is anything wrong?"

"What? Oh, yes. No!" She cleared her throat. "Nothing's wrong."

"Are you sure?" He was already shrugging into his jacket, ready to rush out the door. Something wasn't right.

"Of course I'm sure. I was just trying to save my lamp."

"Save your lamp?" The nonsequitur mysteriously relieved him, and he sank back into his chair.

"Yes. I managed that okay, but I think I killed the clock. No, no, it's alive."

"Am I supposed to understand any of this?"

Her warm laugh fluttered through the telephone and settled somewhere in his chest.

"Not really."

He could visualize her smile and smiled back. "I can't tell you how reassuring that is."

She laughed again. "Just put it down to another accident. Only this time, it was between me and my lamp. Then the lamp hit the clock and—why are you calling?"

"I wanted to make sure you got home safely."

"I'm perfectly fine, as you can tell. But thank you for calling. It was nice of you to be concerned."

"Nice, hell!" Anger at the sudden coolness in her tone pushed out his relief. "I shouldn't have let you drive home alone in the first place. I should have picked you up and seen you home."

"I didn't want you to pick me up."

"I know that. I just don't like it. Anything might have happened. A flat tire, engine trouble, muggers—" He tried to blot out the pictures forming in his mind but couldn't completely let go. "Why did it take you so long to get home?"

"Long? Nick, I was half-asleep when you called. I'd been home almost an hour."

"You were asleep? At ten o'clock?"

There was a brief pause. "Well, not exactly asleep. Just close to it."

It hit him then. "So . . . you're in bed?"

"Yes, Nick. That's usually where I do my sleeping."

"Oh, well, then . . . why didn't you answer my other calls?" He barely managed to choke out the question. His body was going crazy at the vision of Jordan sprawled seductively across her bed.

"I don't know. I guess I must have been in the shower."

His chest constricted. "The shower." Her body would have been wet and glistening. And then she would have patted each delectable curve dry and slipped into . . . He felt like a fool, but he had to know. "What are you wearing?"

She chuckled. "Forget it, Nick. I'm not about to carry on like some sex-starved teenager."

"Ah, come on, Jordan." He tried to make his tone as playful as hers, though his body definitely didn't consider this a game. "Tell me what you wear to bed."

"No way, buster."

"Then just tell me what color it is."

"Not on your life!"

"Is it long or short?"

She didn't answer, but he could hear her breathing; it was fast, just like his. He shifted in his chair, so uncomfortable he thought he'd explode. "You do sleep in something, don't you?"

"I'm not telling you a thing," she said in a no-nonsense voice. "I can't decide if you're an aging juvenile delinquent, or just a dirty old man."

He laughed, delighted. He loved it when she got sassy. "Not dirty," he informed her. "And thirty-three certainly isn't old. Just lusty."

"Same difference."

"You can't be serious. If you really believe that, I'm going to make it my personal responsibility to teach you the difference. Very thoroughly, and very slowly."

The way her breathing altered told him she understood. He could imagine how she looked, her expressive face open and vulnerable.

"How did we get into this conversation?" she asked, sounding slightly flustered.

"You brought it up," he said, wanting her to share the responsibility, and the fun, of where they'd been.

"In a completely innocent way!"

"Tell you what. Let me come over and check out your night wear, just to give me a little peace of mind, and I'll try my best to keep things on a platonic level. Cross my heart."

"Now that's really pathetic, Nick."

"Then how about letting me check out your apartment for prowlers? That's what I would have done if you'd let me see you home."

"It's a little late for that! I'd be murdered in my bed long before you got here."

"This conversation could ruin my reputation. I'll just have to work harder to convince you I'm a totally fascinating, wickedly exciting man. I'm adding it to the list of things I need to teach you."

"List?"

"Don't you remember? I'm going to teach you the difference between lusty and dirty. And now I'm going to have to teach you just how exciting I can be." His voice lowered as he thought of all the ways he wanted to show her. "But you needn't worry," he whispered. "I promise to be a very thorough teacher."

Her shaky sigh was all the encouragement he needed.

"Think about that tonight," he said softly. "And remember—I always keep my promises."

Four

The small crowd of people milling outside her door should have warned her, but nothing could have prepared her. Jordan wove through the crowd to her office, sleepy, out of breath, and, thanks to two alarm clocks, only a little late. For a minute she thought—hoped—she was still dreaming. Her office looked like Forest Lawn on Memorial Day. Flowers, in baskets and bouquets of every size, shape, and color filled the room.

"Oh, Jordan!" Sally Becker's ample bosom heaved with excitement as she all but shouted, "Isn't it romantic? I've never seen so many flowers!"

Other voices chimed in as the small group followed her into the room, each one giving his or her idea of which was the most beautiful arrangement, which the most exquisite flower. Jordan was speechless. Speechless and embarrassed.

How could he? was all she could think. How could he? She knew who'd done this. She could picture him planning and plotting with that . . .

that grin on his face. He had to have known what a ruckus this would cause. She sank into her chair and stared helplessly around the room.

"It must be love," a male voice pronounced.

"He sure must be rich!"

"Maybe they're for Clay."

"Who's the guy, Jordan?"

She tried to smile, but she knew the effort must look as plastic as it felt. She would kill him, she decided, as she listened to the speculation mount. She would cheerfully kill him. Didn't he realize what people would think when they found out who sent the flowers? How could he expose her to that kind of speculation?

"Okay, folks. Showtime's over!" Nick's voice boomed above the noise. "I'm sure you all have work to do."

Jordan remained silent as the group filed out. She didn't trust herself to speak. She didn't look at Nick either. Not until everyone else was gone.

She heard the door click shut and knew she and Nick were alone. Only then did she allow herself to look around. She had to move an arrangement of irises out of the way before she could see him. He was bending over, smelling another bouquet; one with rosebuds, daisies, and jonquils, with baby's breath tucked discreetly throughout.

"Pretty, aren't they?" Nick commented casually.

Jordan's blood started to boil.

"Nice selection," he noted, with a tentative smile.

She closed her eyes and breathed deeply. She would not scream, she would not scream. She would not—

"I think flowers say so much. Don't you?"

Her eyes flew open and she glared at him, still not trusting her voice.

"Now, Jordan. Don't look at me like that. This was all a mistake, you know."

That did it.

"A mistake! A room full of flowers is a mistake!"

"It was only supposed to be a bouquet of flowers. One bouquet. That's all." His tone held not the slightest twinge of remorse.

"One bouquet?" she repeated disbelievingly.

He nodded. "That's right. I called Arnold at five o'clock this morning and told him I wanted a bouquet of every kind of flower he had on hand delivered to the station before eight-thirty this morning. I meant one bouquet. Just . . . one."

Some of her anger ebbed. "You woke someone named Arnold at five o'clock? For flowers?"

"Sure. We're old friends. I always get my flowers from him. His voice faltered as he realized his mistake. "I mean I—" He looked away. "I guess Arnold misunderstood."

"Rather a costly misunderstanding, wouldn't you say, Nick?"

He shrugged. "I just wanted to send you some flowers."

It suddenly struck Jordan as funny, and she tried to bite back a smile but failed. The smile became a giggle and the giggle, laughter.

"Tell me one thing," she asked when she'd regained enough control to phrase a logical sentence.

"What?"

"What in the world am I going to do with all these flowers? I don't suppose you can take them back to Arnold?"

"No, I don't suppose I could. In fact, when I

called him about the, uh, misunderstanding, he wasn't the least bit sympathetic."

"But it's such an expensive error."

He gave her an amused glance. "Well that's a first. Women aren't usually concerned about how much money they cost me."

"I am *not* most women," she retorted.

"I'm well aware of how special you are." he assured her. "And don't worry about this. Arnold and I are always trying to gouge each other," he continued. "He got me this time, but I'll get him at the next fund-raiser, when he'll end up contributing all the floral arrangements. It's just a little harmless fun."

She eyed the overflowing room. Harmless fun, huh? She'd hate to see what happened when those two guys got serious over money.

"So what do we do with the flowers?" she asked. "I can't take all these—" she made a sweeping gesture with her hand, "—home. There're just too many."

Nick's forehead puckered as he considered the problem. A smile lit his face. "Got it!" He walked around the desk and sifted through the assortment of bouquets until he uncovered the telephone. He winked at Jordan and punched an interoffice number.

"Harley? Nick. I need one of the vans. No. Empty. Thirty minutes? Okay." He hung up the phone and smiled. "All taken care of."

"How? What are you going to do?"

"Phoenix Children's Hospital," he explained simply.

"Oh, Nick! What a wonderful idea!"

"I have lots of wonderful ideas."

His gaze was warm and filled with a hint of something she was hesitant to put a name to. He leaned down and brushed his lips over hers in an exploring kiss. It was soft, and sweet, and tender. And it was enough to start a slow melting of her bones. She felt as if she were drifting, floating on a billowing white cloud. He hesitated, then his mouth moved firmly over hers. He parted his lips, coaxing her to respond, and she was helpless not to follow his lead. His tongue crossed the threshold of her mouth, tracing the inner edge of her lips with slow thoroughness before easing deeper inside.

She loved the taste of him, his warm, earthy scent, the feel of his hand as it encircled the back of her neck. She wanted to let the feelings blossom, the moments to linger, but she forced herself to pull away. She opened her eyes to find his turbulent gaze sweeping over her face.

Nick studied her luminous green eyes and kiss-tinted mouth until his hunger for her sharpened like a knife in his belly. He moved to take her lips again, craving their sweet response.

"No, Nick," she cautioned, leaning back in her chair.

She took a ragged breath, and he had the comfort of knowing her refusal wasn't any easier for her to say than it was for him to hear.

"I think we've given the office enough to gossip about for one day."

"I don't give a damn about that," he stated bluntly. "Life is too short for playing hide-and-seek with what you want. You have to reach out and take it."

He watched her for a moment, trying to see if he'd reached her. Then he straightened, still holding her gaze.

"I'm trying not to go too fast, Jordan, I really am. It's just awfully damn hard."

Before she could answer, he smiled and looked around the room. "Pick out which arrangement you want to keep and put it under your desk until after Harley and I have moved out the rest. That is, if you want to keep one."

His expression held such hopeful skepticism that Jordan would have kept every single bouquet if it were the least bit feasible.

"Of course I'll keep one." She watched his skepticism turn to pleasure before she gave her attention to the flowers. "But they're all so beautiful, it will take me a few minutes to decide."

She scanned the room until her gaze fell on the arrangement Nick had toyed with earlier.

"This one," she said, carefully lifting the bouquet, which was set in a lovely wicker basket.

Nick's face glowed. "That's my favorite too." He drew his finger along the side of her face. "See? We're perfect for each other." He planted a quick kiss on the the tip of her nose and walked to the door. He opened it and was halfway out before he looked over his shoulder and told her, "But then, I knew that the moment I first looked at you."

For just a moment, he seemed surprised, as if he hadn't intended to say that. Then he smiled, and the surprise was hers, because she felt that maybe, just maybe, he meant it.

• • •

"If I weren't so happily married, I'd sure strut my stuff in front of those Estevis brothers," Sally said and grinned, before attacking her salad.

Jordan and Delia Harris, a technician with KJTX, looked at each other and burst out laughing.

"If I had what you've got," Delia mourned, eyeing Sally's voluptuous figure, "I'd be strutting it, married or not."

"That pretty little ring you're wearing tells me Mark likes what you've got just fine," Sally said, taking the ribbing over her hourglass dimensions with her usual good nature. "And Jordan seems to have someone on the hook," she added, referring, Jordan was sure, to the flower incident.

Sally turned to Jordan and pulled her face into a sad expression. "Come on, Jordan. Who is he? I might die of curiosity if you don't tell."

Jordan laughed but didn't answer. Sally was warmhearted and easygoing, but she was also the office grapevine.

"How long till the wedding?" Jordan asked Delia, trying to get Sally's attention off her love life. Though Nick had become much more circumspect in his pursuit, he spent what she considered an inordinate amount of time with her, going over daily schedules and using any other excuse he could come up with to solidify their growing relationship. She just wasn't ready to admit to anyone else that there was a relationship. Not yet.

Delia's face glowed as she smiled in answer to Jordan's question. "Only five more weeks, and then I'll be Mrs. Mark Carerra."

"Mark's a great guy," Jordan said. She liked the quiet, efficient cameraman.

"It's too bad you can't have a real honeymoon," Sally added sympathetically. "But since you just got hired, you don't have any vacation time. I don't suppose Mark would want to honeymoon without you."

"Can you two keep a secret?" Delia asked, with barely suppressed excitement.

"Cross my heart and hope to die," Sally promised, lifting her right hand and making an X in the center of her chest.

"My lips are sealed," Jordan added, wondering what Delia's big secret was.

"Swear, Sally," Delia insisted.

"Okay, okay! I swear!"

"On your mother's grave."

Sally rolled her eyes, but made the promise.

"A few days ago Mr. Estevis called me and Mark into his office and gave us"—Delia paused dramatically—"two round-trip tickets to Acapulco and a reservation at the Acapulco Princess!" She beamed with delight. "I'm so excited I can hardly stand it!"

"That's wonderful!" Sally and Jordan said in unison.

"But that's not the best part. Well, maybe it is, but, oh golly, it's just all so exciting! He also told us not to show our faces around here for two weeks after the wedding! Imagine! He's letting us take our vacation six months early!"

"I knew Steven Estevis was a sweet guy," Delia said sagely. "He may have made a lot of changes in the station, but they've all been for the better."

"Oh, no!" Delia gasped. "It wasn't Steven! It was the other one. Nicholas."

"Mr. Tall, Dark, and Mysterious did that!" Sally's eyes rounded in surprise, and Jordan knew hers looked just the same.

"Yeah, Old Intimidator himself. You could have knocked me over with a feather. He's so handsome, but he scares the bejabbers out of me. The way he looks at you with those big black eyes of his, as if he could see right through you."

Jordan was silent. She knew what Delia meant about Nick's eyes. She'd seen that cold, hard look. But she'd also seen them bright with humor and warm with desire.

"Why the big secret?" Sally asked.

Delia chuckled. "He said he didn't want the word to get around. He didn't want all his employees running off and getting married, hoping they'd get a free trip. But you know what I think?" Her voice became hushed. "I think he just doesn't want anyone to know what a romantic he is."

Jordan smiled privately. She already knew.

Five

"Don't do this to me today," Jordan pleaded with the lock to her apartment, giving the key a sharp twist only to feel it stick again. She set her purse on the concrete slab of her entry and attacked the door, turning the key with one hand and jiggling the doorknob with the other. "Open, you crummy hunk of—"

"Looks like you could use some help."

She whirled at the sound of the unmistakable voice, her heart thundering in shocked surprise.

"Good Lord, Nick!" She pressed a hand to her throat, hoping her suddenly boneless knees wouldn't buckle. "I didn't hear you walk up."

"You were too busy talking to the door." He reached around her, filling the air with an intoxicating scent of masculinity and spice, and twisted the key.

She watched with disgust as the lock gave easily and the door swung open. Must be a female, she reasoned, glaring at the metal plate that had given her nothing but trouble since the day she'd moved in. "It never worked that easily for me."

"You just didn't talk to it in the right tone."

"Yeah," she agreed, retrieving her purse. "Baritone."

His eyes crinkled with the smile that lifted his perfectly carved lips, and the usual fluttering of her heart became a wild banging. She dropped her gaze from his bewitching mouth to what should have been safer ground, and found dark chest hairs peeking boldly from the V of his open-neck shirt. Her breathing stopped while she visualized dense black hair tapering to his lean waist and trailing down . . .

She snapped her attention away from the tantalizing picture. "What are you doing here, Nick?"

"Gambling that you'll have dinner with me."

"Tonight?"

"You haven't eaten yet, have you?"

"Well, no, but—"

"Good!" His expression looked boyishly eager. "I'll be right back."

Before she could say another word, he was jogging down the sidewalk to his car in the smooth, rhythmic pace of a well-toned athlete. He opened the car door and pulled out a shallow, square box that Jordan recognized as coming from her favorite pizza place. Her stomach growled happily. Weak! she railed silently, watching his equally rhythmic return. She was weak.

"Hang on just a sec." He maneuvered around her, stepping into the apartment. After setting the pizza box in the kitchen, he began walking through her apartment, flipping on lights, opening closet doors.

"What are you doing?" Jordan asked, exasperated.

"Would you prefer to check for your own prowlers?"

"As a matter of fact," she started, then realized the futility of her objections. She sighed. "Help yourself."

He smiled victoriously and continued his prowler hunt while she went into the kitchen, listening with a curious pleasure to the sounds of doors being opened and closed. That last click would be the bedroom closet, she deduced, grateful that her closet was as neat as the rest of her apartment. She gave a light shrug. Neatness was a breeze when possessions were scarce.

"All clear."

She looked over her shoulder and caught him eyeing her with curiosity.

"Lived here long?"

It was a typical reaction from someone seeing her home for the first time, but for some reason, hearing it from him made her defensive. "About six months." She tried to concentrate on the delicious aroma escaping from the pizza box. The neighborhood was a little run-down, but she was proud of the fact she was making it on her own. She might not have much, but it was all hers.

"Do you belong to some religious sect that doesn't believe in material possessions?"

She stiffened. "Nope. I just don't like furnished apartments, and I'm very fussy about what I spend my money on."

He nodded. "I can see that."

She sighed and took two plates from the cabinet. "But you don't understand it."

"Sure I do," he said. "It's just surprising to walk

into someone's apartment and find one couch, one bed, and one dresser."

"And a television, nightstand, and two bar stools," she amended.

He followed her around the kitchen, taking the forks and glasses from her and setting them next to the plates.

"What are we drinking?" he asked as he opened the refrigerator.

Her uneasiness mounted when she saw him eyeing the scanty contents of her fridge. In probing through her possessions, Nick seemed to be probing through her life, and finding it equally barren. She shouldn't feel defensive, she knew. She wanted people to make themselves at home; she preferred a relaxed informality. Besides, there was no one to distract or entertain Nick while she went about her work. They were completely—alone.

The idea dropped to her stomach, solidifying her nebulous tension. Alone. No interruptions, no business. No waiters. No getting up and leaving if the situation got a little too tense. Alone. In her apartment.

Nick cleared his throat and peered at her from over the refrigerator door. "I know it's a big decision, but could you let me know before the pizza gets cold?"

"Wh . . . I'm sorry?" She struggled to get her racing thoughts back under control.

"Milk, orange juice, or some kind of brown stuff in a smiley-faced Kool-Aid pitcher?"

"Oh!" Her laugh was too loud. She'd meant to throw that out days ago, but kept forgetting. "That's tea."

He looked disbelieving.

"Kind of old tea."

He stared at the pitcher, his expression of disbelief turning to one of disgust. "That's not old, Jordan. That's decayed."

"I didn't know I'd be entertaining this evening."

Nick shut the refrigerator door, stepping necessarily closer with the movement. Her embarrassed pride slammed head-on with sensual awareness. Self-confidence evaporated.

He took the pitcher and dumped the contents in the sink. "I guess we'll have to settle for milk or water. Somehow pizza and orange juice just doesn't quite make it. Tea would have been better. Or beer. I could make a quick run to the store and get some."

Each word was a wound to her fragile ego, reminding her of all the times she'd failed to please before. First her parents, always finding fault with her less than perfect decorum. Then Clark, accusing her of being too uptight, too rigid in her moral beliefs. Now Nick.

"Or you could take your pizza and go find someone who has a house full of furniture and a pitcher of fresh tea and a six-pack of—"

"What is it with you?" His words were clipped, his face taut. "I wasn't complaining or criticizing. I thought we were getting along great, and then, wham! You jump off the deep end. Is it me?" he asked, ignoring her attempted protest. "Am I so uncouth, so reprehensible, that you can't abide the thought of being with me? I've been tiptoeing around for days, trying to get through that wall of yours, and just when I think things are okay, you—"

"I know!" she all but yelled to stop his verbal barrage. "I . . . know."

They stared at each other. He, visibly working to douse his temper. She, trying to come to grips with her own confused emotions.

"It's crazy, Nick," she finally managed. "I can't seem to reconcile my attraction to you with the idea that you're absolutely wrong for me. I feel like . . ." She sighed. "I don't know. I guess I take my frustration out on you. I . . . I'm sorry."

"What makes you so sure I'm wrong for you?" he asked, genuinely baffled. "You know next to nothing about me."

"I know your reputation with women."

"What reputation?" His temper flared again. "Do I beat them? Murder them? Leave them pregnant in the snow? What the hell are you talking about?"

"You . . . you . . . have them." The statement sounded ludicrous even to her. "Lots of them," she added, as if that would make her objection more plausible.

"Oh?" His eyebrows lifted. "One at a time or all together?"

"How should I know?"

"Exactly! How should you know anything about me and my so-called women? Do you know them? Have you talked to them? Did they tell you I was some sort of monster?"

She felt trapped. Searching for a refuge, she spotted the pizza and walked around the kitchen counter that served as a bar, eased onto one of the stools, and picked up a piece. She could feel Nick watching her every move.

"Well?" he demanded.

"Newspapers," she mumbled.

"Ah, I see," he nodded sagely. "You follow the gossip columns. Those paragons of truth and factual reporting. Heaven forbid a journalist should question their veracity."

She took a bite of lukewarm pizza, trying to put off the inevitable. He had her, and she knew it. "Maybe you'd better start eating before this gets too cold," she said, looking down at the food.

She heard the second bar stool slide from under the counter.

"What do gossip columns and women I may or may not have known before I met you have to do with us?"

She took a deep breath and turned to face him.

"Clark asked me the same thing once. After we'd been married a couple of years. I tried not to believe what I read, what I heard; but when I caught him in bed with my best friend, I knew I had to get out. I couldn't take it anymore." Surprisingly, the confession didn't hurt. But Nick nearly choked when she added, "You remind me of him.

"Clark was handsome, successful, and very . . . popular with women. He was so charming and fun. He made me feel so . . . happy. I fell hard and fast and didn't come up for air till the honeymoon was over. By the time I understood what his lifestyle entailed, it was too late. I couldn't fit in with his world, and he couldn't settle into mine.

"Everything I know about you, or think I know," she amended, "is too familiar. I don't want to become involved with another Romeo . . . ahhh . . . man like that."

He studied her quietly, a curious softening in

his eyes. He put down his napkin and captured her hand, not speaking until her gaze met his.

"That explains a lot," he said evenly. "But it doesn't change a thing. I'm not Clark, and I resent being compared to him." His grip on her hand tightened, and his voice became stronger. "He was a complete bastard to treat you like that. I have my faults like anyone else, but when I was married, I was never unfaithful. Ever. So do me the courtesy of dropping that comparison."

He released her hand and reached for a slice of pizza. "As for the rest"—he gave a nonchalant shrug—"I'm willing to give you a break if you'll do the same for me."

"Give *me* a break?" Her voice cracked in amazement.

"Yes," he answered smoothly. "I'll ignore all my misgivings and give us a chance, if you'll do the same."

"Misgivings?"

He swung around to face her. "I'm not usually attracted to your type, you know." He punctuated his statement with a look of wide-eyed candor.

"Oh?" She laughed, slightly taken aback. "What type do you prefer? Blonde? Brunette?"

"No," he said around his food. "I usually prefer women who know exactly who they are. Who aren't afraid to reach out and take what they want—in both their professional and their *personal* lives. You're a tiger when it comes to your career, and I admire that. But you're a real chicken when it comes to anything personal."

"And what makes you think I'm afraid?" she asked, picking up her own pizza. She felt a bit nonplussed by his analysis, but comfortable—refreshingly so—with their open communication.

"Everything. The frequent moves and job changes. The way you flash hot and cold with me. Even your lack of possessions. I don't think you know what you want, and you're afraid to reach out for anything in case you get burned."

She considered his words. "You mean because I prefer to look before I leap?" She drained her glass of milk, picked up her fork and plate, and took them to the sink.

"It's okay to look," he acknowledged, picking up his own dishes. "As long as you don't freeze up while trying to make a decision. You look, then you either jump or back off."

"I believe I tried that with you." She smiled. "You won't seem to take no for an answer."

"That's because there is no on your lips, but—"

"There's yes, yes in my eyes," she completed for him, not the least upset in making the admission. It was true.

"Often enough to make me want to see which way the pendulum swings."

She faltered over that one. "I still don't know, Nick. Being attracted to you just isn't enough."

"I understand that. Now." He laughed ruefully. "I'll admit I'm used to women who don't ask for more than that, but"—he paused—"I don't know. Maybe it's not enough for me anymore, either."

Until she felt the warmth of his skin beneath her hand, she wasn't aware she'd reached up to smooth the troubled frown from his face. The moment she touched him, her senses fired with awareness. A matching flame leaped in his eyes.

"Time, Nick," she breathed. "Give it time."

He gave a ghost of a smile and covered her hand with his own, wanting her so much he hurt. "I think I should give you fair warning that I'm not exactly famous for my patience."

She nodded, too preoccupied with the feel of his skin moving beneath her hand to speak. His jaw was so strong under the warm, mobile flesh.

He inhaled deeply and turned his mouth into her palm. His fiery gaze held hers as he pressed a brief, urgent kiss at the base of her fingers.

"I think I've been exercising enormous restraint since you came barreling into my life. See what you do to my respiration with no more than a touch?" He lifted her hand and placed it on his chest. She could feel his heart thundering under the solid mass of muscle. His chest heaved in deep, shaky breaths.

"Then we have a serious problem," she said. "You seem to have an uncanny knack"—she watched as her fingers spread and began searching for warm flesh—"for taking my wonderfully placid nature and—" she swallowed—"turning it into a tempest." She found the opening of his shirt and felt his skin beneath the wiry tufts of raven hair. "I think we could be in for some real trouble."

His need for self-restraint was almost palpable. "Are you putting it to a test?"

Her gaze lifted to his, and she saw the hunger there. She hadn't been conscious of what her sinuous exploration was doing to him, she'd only been aware of her own pleasure.

When she tried to pull away, he stopped her, pressing her palm flat against his chest.

"Too late." A small smile played across his lips. "I think I just flunked."

Then he pulled her closer, lowering his mouth to hers. His lips were warm, exploring softly as they tested and teased her waiting mouth. She could taste the desire he held in check, feel the restraint in his tender probing. His masculinity enveloped her in a cloak of longing so strong she was shaken by its intensity. She didn't dare reach out to hold him. She was afraid if she did, she might never let him go.

Slowly, his mouth left hers, and she opened her eyes to the black velvet of his gaze.

"I think I'd better go," he said quietly. "Unless you have a lot more willpower than I do."

"How much will it take?"

A slow smile lifted his lips. "Do you have any reinforced steel?"

"Fresh out." She sagged weakly against him.

"Well, then . . ."

"Well . . ." she sighed, letting her eyes drift shut. She knew she was making it difficult for him. But she felt so good in his arms, so right. And she was certain, at least for now, that she could trust him. She snuggled a little closer.

"I'm leaving now," he said, not moving a muscle. "Right now."

"Okay," she said dreamily.

"I'll see you tomorrow night." He still didn't move.

"Okay."

When he did leave, several minutes later, she'd already begun to miss him.

The next night he beat her home. He was waiting with a bucket of fried chicken, a liter of cola, and a big smile. The smile wavered when he got a good look at her.

"You look beat," he said sympathetically, trading her the chicken for her keys.

"A little." She leaned against the wall while he opened the door, then followed him inside. "You left just when things started getting really crazy." She had to raise her voice when he went through his prowler check. "You can't imagine how wild it was giving a tour of the station to twenty-two second-graders." She sighed. "Remind me never to become a schoolteacher."

He came back to the kitchen and patted one of the bar stools. "Sit. I'll serve the meal."

She gladly relinquished the chore, taking the opportunity to watch him while he worked. Despite her fatigue, she couldn't help but notice how handsome he looked in his chinos and casual shirt.

With an economy of movement he rounded up plates and glasses, dished up chicken, cole slaw, and rolls, and topped it off with a fizzing glass of iced cola.

"You're a prince," she said, smiling, as he joined her at the bar.

His grin was cocky. "I know. I was wondering how long it would take you to figure it out."

"I think it happened right after I kissed you." She scrunched up her forehead. "Yeah, I'm pretty sure that was the last time I heard you r-r-ribit."

"You're a wicked woman, Jordan Donner."

"I know. I was wondering how long it would take you to notice."

They finished their meal in companionable silence, and Nick was quick to clean up the kitchen.

"How about some TV?" he said as he made his way to the living room. He stopped abruptly and cast her a worried frown. "Or are you too tired?"

She *was* tired. It had been a long, hot day, and she'd planned on going to bed early. "We're showing a wonderful old movie right after the news."

"*Sergeant York*?" His eyes glowed. "I knew you were a woman after my own heart. Not only do you like pizza and chicken and frogs, but you like old movies." He pressed crossed hands over his heart and staggered to the couch. "I think I'm in love."

She laughed at his antics, as she knew he expected her to, but his words elicited a familiar longing. Was it possible for love to be so simple? It sounded so nice, so uncomplicated, so . . . unconditional.

She blanked out the sentimental imaginings. "Why don't you turn on the television while I go change?"

"Into something more comfortable?"

"Into jeans."

He forced an exaggerated sigh. "I knew it was too good to be true."

When she returned to the living room, Nick was engrossed in the news. He'd found the paper and pen she kept in the kitchen for making shopping lists and was taking notes on the broadcast. Over his shoulder she read, "Cut to Tom—sloppy, tighten intro."

She settled herself on the opposite end of the couch and started watching critically. When the piece she and Clayton had edited came on, she tensed when she heard his pen scratching across the paper.

"Good spot," Nick said when it was over.

Jordan smiled to herself. Clayton would be sure to remind Nick that that was her story.

Something she'd been wondering about popped into her mind.

"Were you and Clayton in the service together?"

Nick was silent while he put the paper and pen on the floor near the couch, then said, "He was my C.O."

"You fly?" She was amazed. Clayton, she knew, had commanded a helicopter unit.

He stiffened. "Not anymore."

"How could you give it up? It's so fantastic. You're so free up there, so—"

"I know all about those feelings. I had them once. I don't anymore."

"But—"

"Let's just say I went up one too many times."

She hated what she saw in his eyes: sadness, anger, resignation. She knew he was thinking of his friend and she wished she could comfort him, but he looked away, uncomfortable under her scrutiny. She let the matter drop.

"Almost time for the movie," he announced. The lightness in his voice sounded forced.

"How 'bout some popcorn?" She motioned him to stay seated and went to the kitchen. When she returned, Nick was semireclining, his legs stretched lengthwise on the couch, a cushion tucked between his back and the armrest.

"Don't go into a panic," he said, when he saw her eyeing him. "I'll share."

That was what she was afraid of.

He patted the empty space between his spread legs. "Come on," he urged at her obvious reluctance. "If you don't fit, we'll move."

It was the challenge that got her, she insisted to herself, not the inviting picture of being comfortably ensconced between his thighs.

At first she couldn't relax. She was too aware of his legs pressed against her hips, the way he had to keep his arms around her in order to reach the popcorn nestled in her lap. But eventually she settled in, smiling privately when he pressed her head back so she could use his chest for a pillow.

The deep, even rhythm of his breathing was soothing, his body warm and firm. Her eyelids began to feel heavy, the movie became a soft, black-and-white blur. The next thing she was aware of was a husky voice whispering, "Wake up, Sleeping Beauty. You'll be much more comfortable in bed."

Jordan stirred groggily and snuggled back into his warmth. She didn't want to get up. She was too cozy, too comfortable. She frowned. Shifting her hips, she tried to smooth out a bump near the small of her back. A bump that hadn't been there before.

She heard Nick gasp. "Stop wiggling, Jordan, or I won't be held accountable for my actions."

She froze, her sleep-drugged mind suddenly realizing exactly what that "bump" was. The air felt heavy, the silence thick, until she heard the static buzz of the televison, telling her KJTX had signed off for the night.

How long had she been sleeping? Poor Nick must be miserable. She sat up and turned to him, trying but not quite succeeding in keeping her gaze from straying below his waist. "I'm so sorry, Nick. How awful for you."

He looked at her as if she'd lost her mind, then glanced down. "No one's ever complained before."

She followed his gaze to the obvious bulge in his slacks, then flashed back to his bemused face. She thought for a second she might burst out laughing, but his look of wounded male pride stopped her.

"Not that!" she blurted. "I mean . . ." She tried to get a breath, but her lungs were constricted with sudden embarrassment. "I mean . . ." she gasped, trying not to look at him or his face. "I meant you must have been terribly uncomfortable with me sleeping on you like that for who knows how long and I'm sorry about squashing you. Not . . . not . . ." She couldn't go on.

He started laughing. "Well, thank God for that." He put his hands on her waist and nudged her to her feet. "My ego might never have recovered," he said, standing.

Jordan stepped to the television and switched it off, using the action to try to recover her poise. When she turned to face him, he held out his hand to her.

"Walk me to the door," he said, making her heart do funny things. She couldn't decide if it was fluttering with relief that he was willing to go peacefully when he was so obviously ready to prolong the evening, or if it was turning over in disappointment that he was going. He looked so handsome with his hair all rumpled and his eyes heavy-lidded with sleep . . . or desire. God help her but she wanted him.

Their fingers interlaced, and Jordan reveled in the quiet intimacy of the touch. They walked slowly to the door.

He had to drop her hand when the lock stuck again. It took both of his to manipulate it. "I think I'd better fix this for you," he said, when the door finally gave.

"That's very thoughtful of you, but you don't have to bother. I'll be moving as soon as I can find another apartment."

He scowled. "It would be a lot easier to put in a new lock."

"I'm going to move, regardless."

His scowl deepened. "You're determined to go through with the call-out business, aren't you?"

She nodded, not wanting to say anything that might rouse his temper.

"Then I guess we'd better start looking at apartments over the weekend."

"We? Oh, Nick. I can't ask you to give up your weekend. It might take quite a while and—"

"You're not asking. I'm offering. If you're going to move because of your job, I need to know that you've found a safe location; with doors that work and windows that lock." He paused. "Sunday?"

She started to object, but the thought of being with him again was too appealing. She smiled. "Fine."

He smiled back, a soft, lazy smile, and stepped closer. Body-brushing closer. "Kiss me good night, Jordan," he said, making no move to take her in his arms. He was waiting for her, she knew. Letting her decide. If she refused, he wouldn't pursue.

Nick held his breath, wanting her to give him her mouth. He could seduce her, and God knew he wanted to, but something about her made him hold back. He wanted more than her body. He wanted her trust, he wanted her to know he was more than just another stud on the prowl. And he wanted her to know she aroused more in him than just his manhood.

Jordan tilted her head and lifted to her toes, pressing a hesitant kiss on his lips. She wanted to wrap her arms around him and meld her body with his, her mouth with his. But she held back, unsure.

Nick felt her indecision in the lingering caress of her mouth, and all his good intentions evaporated. Before she could pull away, his arms closed around her. "Kiss me like you mean it," he ordered huskily. "Let me taste you, feel you."

She didn't hesitate. Her arms wrapped around his neck, pulling, pulling, wrapping tighter and tighter until her face was level with his and there was no more than a breath between them. His legs parted to accommodate the length of hers, allowing her to press into him, to feel his hunger.

His mouth covered hers; searing, claiming, taking all she offered, but giving more. Desire rose with renewed urgency, and she savored it. This was a man's kiss, and she received it with a woman's longing, answering each demand of his mouth with one of her own, exchanging intuitive, elemental understandings.

Nick's breathing was erratic when they finally parted, an erotic rhythm that partnered her own. He released her slowly, making the separation bearable only because it was so eloquent. She stood in trembling silence, waiting for sanity to return, praying it wouldn't. It came. Not with the remorse she expected, but with soft, tender comfort. They had shared more than desire with that kiss, more than mere physical assuagement. She had tasted his longing, felt his hunger for more than casual sex. Her kiss had been her own confession, a testament of secret yearnings.

Nick's gaze poured over her, searching. She met it, telling him with her smile she had no regrets. He answered her smile with his eyes; bright, sparkling pools of warm delight. The back of his fingers brushed a butterfly kiss on her cheek as he lifted a lock of hair from her shoulder.

"Will you come to a party with me Saturday night?" he asked, toying with the captured strands.

Caution invaded her enchantment. "A party?"

"At the Brierlys'. Kind of elaborate, I'm afraid, but I'm trapped into going."

Her blood chilled at the mention of the Brierlys', a name at the top of the Phoenix social register. Every word he uttered sounded a death knell over her newfound ease. She shook her head, and he stopped in middescription of the affair.

"Why not? It won't be so bad."

"I know exactly how it will be, Nick. I've been to too many parties like that not to know. And I hated them. I could never relax, never mingle, never fit in. I just don't care who spent the winter in Nice or whose dress cost the most."

He laughed, but that just reinforced her determination. He'd never really understand how much she hated the pretentious one-upmanship.

"It's not the least bit funny, Nick."

"I know that," he assured her, his eyes soft with understanding. "But you'll be with me. I won't let you feel uncomfortable. I'll be by your side every minute."

She steeled herself. "No, Nick."

He raked his fingers through his hair, a gesture she was beginning to know as a sign of frustration.

"I can't get out of it now, Jordan. The Brierlys are expecting me. I have to go, especially with Steven out of town. It's an important contact."

"I understand." She knew all about the social games that were played at these affairs, and all the wheeling and dealing that went on behind the scenes.

Nick's chin jutted stubbornly. "All right, Jordan. But don't think for a minute that this business is any excuse for trying to pull away. You don't like formal parties? Fine. I'll go alone."

Nick stared around the congested room, wishing he were with Jordan. He wanted to touch her, smell her, hear her laughter. Just the thought of her made him hungry. Sweet Lord, she had him in a constant state of arousal. And he was getting damn tired of cold showers and long swims.

A sultry brunette sidled up to him, looking and smelling like the willing woman he knew she was.

"Hi, Nick." Her voice was as low and sexy as her dress. "You don't look like you're having a very good time."

He smiled, forcing the flirtatious wink that used to be so natural. "I always have a good time, Stephanie. You should remember that."

"I do," she murmured. "Quite fondly. Perhaps we should renew our acquaintance somewhere a little more private?"

He remembered her mouth. Hard, greedy, demanding. A peculiar feeling swept him when he thought of other lips, soft and responsive—Jordan's lips—and they made him think of more than just beds and sex. It came softly and stealthily, this prickling awareness, growing just a little stronger each time he thought of her. He'd never considered himself a particularly tender man, but that's what he'd call this new sensation, this almost painful longing. Tenderness.

He felt Stephanie brush against him, her musky perfume a direct assault on his masculinity. He responded, momentarily, then her pale hand stroked his arm, and his heat fled as quickly as it came. He felt restless and bored, and he felt something missing but didn't know what. He just knew he couldn't stand being with Stephanie another minute. He gave her a half-baked excuse, and walked away from the daggers in her gaze.

Jordan listened to the laughter of her friends and tried to concentrate on the game.

"Your turn," Todd reminded her, nudging the die in her direction.

She took her turn, not really paying attention to the trivia question Gary read to her.

"Come on, Jordan," he scolded. "Get your act together."

"Sorry. I guess I'm just a little tired." *And lonesome.* The thought jarred her. She was with her two best friends. She should be having a wonderful time. Instead, all she could think of was Nick, wondering what he was doing, whom he was with.

She tried to imagine herself at the party. Even the thought made her anxious. But damn, she longed to be with him. She felt as lost and confused as she had the first day she'd met him, but the confusion was tighter, harder to fight. She knew her racing pulses and the warm thoughts she carried of him weren't all directly related to physical wanting. She also knew letting herself get involved with him would be emotional suicide. The question was: Would he be worth it?

Six

Jordan stared at the grainy newspaper picture, her gaze frozen on the couple. She couldn't seem to concentrate on anything else, just the picture, the shadowed black-and-white image of Nick, wrapped in an embrace with a beautiful, ice-cool blonde.

The same clammy feeling she'd felt whenever she'd seen photos of Clark in similar poses engulfed her. She tried to fight the wrenching disappointment, but it was like fighting the wind. Her chest ached with breath held too long. Remembered phrases and arguments flitted through her consciousness; Clark's belittling when he was caught red-handed, Nick's assurances that such things had nothing to do with them.

She closed her eyes, trying to put things into perspective. Nick had invited her to a party. She'd declined. He'd found another companion. It was no big deal. Her heart had no right to ache, to feel so betrayed.

The telephone rang, jolting her out of her daze.

The moment she heard Nick's voice, her mood flew up, then crashed down. She felt as if she'd stepped into a broken elevator.

"Where were you last night?" he asked, after a few minutes of strained conversation. "I called you several times from the party, but there was no answer."

He'd called last night? With Golden Girl hanging all over him? Her mood shifted again. "I, uh, I was with friends."

"Friends?" There was a brief silence. "Doing what?"

Not making goo-goo eyes at a camera, that's for sure. "Oh, we had a real exciting night," she said, tring to sound as if she meant it. "I won fifty cents playing poker, and then got my intellect stimulated by Trivial Pursuit."

As soon as she answered, she felt a little spark of anger. He had no right to quiz *her*, when he was the one kissing in front of newspaper photographers.

"Sounds like a lot more fun than I had," he said with a sigh.

"Poor Nick." Her tone was devoid of sympathy. "Trapped at the social event of the season with nothing but a beautiful blonde to break the monotony."

"You saw the picture."

"How could I miss it, being the ace reporter that I am?"

"Before you start jumping to conclusions, let me explain. I've known Carolyn Brierly for years. We're just friends."

"Right." She knew all about friendship.

"Dammit! I knew you'd—" His tirade was abruptly cut off as a male voice called his name. Jordan heard Nick jump all over the poor guy who'd had the misfortune to interrupt. When Nick came back on the line, she could tell that his patience was ending.

"Dammit! This is just perfect! I have to cancel out on you today!"

"Oh?" She tried to sound casual.

"We had some problems here last night, and Steven's due back this afternoon. I just don't see how I can shake loose until this evening."

"It doesn't matter," she lied. What was going on with her? She should feel relieved, not upset.

"The hell it doesn't. I want to see you. What about later tonight?"

"No!" Panic made her voice too loud. "No," she repeated with better control. "I'm going to go ahead and check out some apartments, and then stop by to visit a couple of frien—"

"I know what you're doing. And it's not going to work."

"Doing?"

"You're placing too much importance on that picture; using it as a wedge. I won't let you do it."

The voice broke into the background again, loud and insistent. Nick swore under his breath.

"I have to go now, but I'm not through with you yet. Not by a long shot. We'll settle this tomorrow."

The connection was broken before she had a chance to say a word. But she knew from the tone of his voice that tomorrow would be a day of reckoning.

• • •

Nick slammed down the receiver, all his frustrated anger poured into that simple act. He was not going to let her put those walls back up, not after the tender care he'd used to knock them down. He was tired. Tired of being patient, tired of feeling his insides twisted into tight knots of desire. He wanted her, and, by God, he was going to have her.

The rotor blades of the helicopter churned to a slow stop. Jordan heaved a weary sigh before unbuckling her harness and beginning a quick postflight. Too many restless nights with too little sleep were beginning to catch up with her.

Across the parking lot she saw a lean figure loping toward her. Although the man was tall and dark, she knew instantly it was Steven, not Nick.

Jordan watched Nick's brother sprint across the helipad. His relaxed, loose-jointed gait contrasted with Nick's smoothly controlled aggression. Steven reminded her of a happy puppy looking for a friendly game of chase, while Nick was more like a wolf on the scent, stalking his prey with relentless purpose: Every movement controlled, contained and deadly.

"Welcome back, stranger," she called.

"I'm glad someone's happy to see me." He smiled, and the faint creases on each side of his mouth deepened into dimples. "My own brother hasn't had even two kind words for me since I got in."

"If you want kind words, maybe you should try keeping your brother apprised about certain decisions—like whom you hire."

Steven draped an arm across her shoulders and

led her to the station. "And deprive myself of the pleasure of surprising my wonderful but bullheaded brother?"

Bullheaded? Yes, Jordan thought as they walked to the snack bar and negotiated their way to an empty table. Bullheaded was a fair description of Nick. "Well, your wonderful brother thinks you were suffering from temporary insanity when you hired me."

"Not to worry," he said, getting a chair for her. "Everything's all straightened out."

Somehow she was not comforted. Bullheaded people weren't exactly notorious for changing their minds.

Steven must have seen her skepticism. He smiled cockily. "I'll admit he was upset that I hired you without consulting him first, but you've been doing a great job, and he knows it. Yeah," he said expansively, "old Nick's coming around. It's a little hard for him to drop the strings, but he's doing it. Little by little."

"What strings?"

He smiled wryly. "Nick's used to being in control. Of everything and everyone. KJTX is my first big venture out from under his wings." He looked around the station cafeteria with a proud, possessive gleam in his eyes. "KJTX is my baby. My project. My chance to make a real contribution to Estco. I have so many plans." His eyes grew dreamy for a moment. "Nick accepts that, and he really does want me to make a go of it, but"—he looked at her with resigned acceptance—"he's having a hard time letting go."

"It sounds like he wants all the power for himself."

"No, not power. Responsibility. Since our parents died, he's been head of the family, head of the company. The proverbial big brother. He feels it's still his responsibility to guide me and protect me from failure." His look turned thoughtful. "He's a little too protective sometimes. But it's only because he cares so much." He smiled again. "Sometimes I want to strangle him, but how can I? He's rarely wrong."

She nodded, turning over the protective facet of Nick's personality like a newfound treasure, fighting against using it to excuse his attitude about her flying.

"How about a drink?" Steven asked. "I'll even pay."

She laughed at his magnanimous offer, knowing the fountain drinks were free. He pulled two cups from the dispenser and filled them with ice and soft drinks. From the back, Steven looked so much like Nick. The same blue-black hair that always seemed slightly mussed, the same broad shoulders and trim hips. The same, and yet she felt no thrill, no sensual awareness, no electrical charge when she looked at Steven. She had no doubt that if it were Nick standing there, her heart would be dancing an erotic tango and her eyes would be feverishly skimming every visible surface of his body, and a few that weren't so visible.

"How'd the story go?" Steven asked when he returned with the drinks and settled into a chair.

"Not too well. We were on the wrong side of the mountain to transmit video." She took a long swig of her soft drink and shrugged. "There was a lot of smoke, but the fire had already been corralled, so Mark shot some tape and we headed back."

Steven nodded in understanding. "That's the way it happens sometimes. Not every alert pans out."

"I know. But that's not going to win me any points with Nick."

"On the contrary. Using good sense always makes points with me."

Nick's deep baritone came from behind her, and Jordan looked around in surprise. Her gaze collided with his as he moved to stand near her chair, and she knew her heart was going to leap out of her chest. She hated—and loved—the feelings that pulsed through her whenever she saw him. How could she use logic and reason to discourage him when she felt so much more alive, so much more in tune with herself, whenever he was near? Just the sound of his voice could unleash senses and feelings that were dormant only moments before.

"See, Jordan?" Steven reached across the table and patted her hand. "I told you not to worry. I've convinced Nick that you're the greatest thing to hit the airwaves since color TV."

Nick frowned at the sight of Steven's hand resting on Jordan's.

"And I thought I'd convinced you to leave Jordan to me," he said, his face devoid of any expression.

The brothers exchanged unreadable glances, then Steven's gaze followed the direction of Nick's, coming to a stop on his own hand, still resting on top of Jordan's. His eyes widened, and he laughed with delight. "I love it! I love it! You're actually pulling that tough-guy bit on me!"

Jordan looked from Steven's laugh-reddened face to Nick's. She couldn't tell if he was ready to scowl or starting to grin.

"Cut it out," Nick ordered in a low voice. But his eyes began to twinkle, and the tight line of his mouth eased into a smile.

"Right!" Steven gave Jordan a playful wink and made an eleborate show of removing his hand from hers. "Don't worry, Nick." He pushed his chair away from the table and stood. "I wouldn't dream of moving in on your lady."

Jordan felt her mouth drop open.

"Smile for the people," Nick's low voice instructed her as Steven sauntered off. "They're watching us."

Her gaze followed Nick's and she flashed a vacant smile at the faces turned toward them. When she saw the speculative looks passing between the employees, the fog in her brain dissipated and she was uneasy.

"Don't worry about them." His mouth was dangerously near as he helped her from the chair, then maneuvered her out the door. "What they think doesn't matter."

"And just what are they thinking?"

Nick ignored her question. "Would you quit balking and come on?" He took her hand and pulled her down the hall.

"Where are we going?" she wondered aloud, amazed by her lack of resistance.

He answered her question by guiding her into the film library. He didn't stop inside the door but led her past the first three rows, down an aisle,

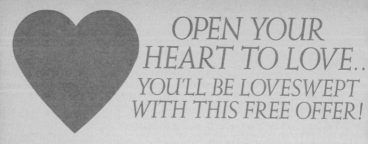

OPEN YOUR HEART TO LOVE...
YOU'LL BE LOVESWEPT WITH THIS FREE OFFER!

HERE'S WHAT YOU GET:

1. **FREE! SIX NEW LOVESWEPT NOVELS!** You get 6 beautiful stories filled with passion, romance, laughter, and tears...exciting romances to stir the excitement of falling in love... again and again.

2. **FREE! A BEAUTIFUL MAKEUP CASE WITH A MIRROR THAT LIGHTS UP!** What could be more useful than a makeup case with a mirror that lights up*? Once you open the tortoise-shell finish case, you have a choice of brushes...for your lips, your eyes, and your blushing cheeks.

*(batteries not included)

3. **SAVE! MONEY-SAVING HOME DELIVERY!** Join the Loveswept at-home reader service and we'll send you 6 new novels each month. You always get 15 days to preview them before you decide. Each book is yours for only $2.09 — a savings of 41¢ per book.

4. **BEAT THE CROWDS!** You'll always receive your Loveswept books before they are available in bookstores. You'll be the first to thrill to these exciting new stories.

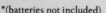

BE LOVESWEPT TODAY — JUST COMPLETE, DETACH AND MAIL YOUR FREE-OFFER CARD.

FREE – LIGHTED MAKEUP CASE!
FREE – 6 LOVESWEPT NOVELS!

- NO OBLIGATION
- NO PURCHASE NECESSARY

(DETACH AND MAIL CARD TODAY.)

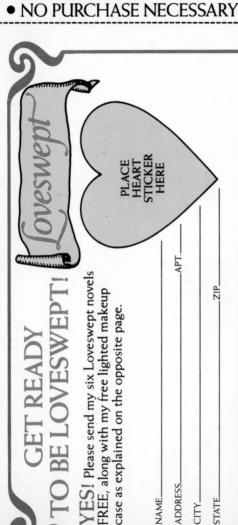

GET READY TO BE LOVESWEPT!

YES! Please send my six Loveswept novels FREE, along with my free lighted makeup case as explained on the opposite page.

NAME _____

ADDRESS _____ APT. _____

CITY _____

STATE _____ ZIP _____

10355

MY "NO RISK" GUARANTEE:

There's no obligation to buy — the free gifts are mine to keep. I may preview each subsequent shipment for 15 days. If I don't want it, I simply return the books within 15 days and owe nothing. If I keep them I will pay just $12.50 (I save $2.50 off the retail price for 6 books) plus postage and handling and any applicable sales tax.

BRj

Prices subject to change. Orders subject to approval.

REMEMBER!
- The free books and gift are mine to keep!
- There is no obligation!
- I may preview each shipment for 15 days!
- I can cancel anytime!

then turned to his left, and zigzagged through several more aisles. They finally reached a small, shadowed hollow at the far side of the room.

Jordan felt the cool, hard surface of the wall against her back as Nick gently nudged her deeper into the recess. He planted his hand near her shoulder, barricading her with his arm and sheltering her with his body.

"I wanted to say good-bye in private," he said, searching her face.

"Good-bye?" She heard the slight quiver in her voice. Leaving? Nick was leaving? She closed her eyes and turned her face away, trying to hide her sadness. Fool, she chided herself. Fool. Fool!

"Hey." He touched her cheek with a light caress, then slid his fingers into her hair, tilting her face to his. "It's business, Jordan."

She forced herself to look at him. He was so breathtakingly handsome. Eyes as black as a starless night, mouth so sensual, so inviting. She was a fool, but no matter how much she wished she could deny it, she wanted him to stay. She wanted him.

"Jordan?" His dark eyes clouded, and a frown creased his forehead. Then his expression brightened.

"You don't want me to go, do you?" he whispered, his heart pounding at the discovery. She wanted him. His eyes closed in relief and delight. At long last, she wanted him and she was ready to admit it, to herself and to him. It was there in her eyes, in her disappointment.

Jordan faked a smile. "I . . . I'm just surprised you're leaving today," she said, "I should have realized as soon as I saw Steven this morning that you weren't needed here any longer. Of course you'll want to get back to your other concerns." The plastic smile stretched further. "Well, good-bye, Nick. It's been . . . interesting."

His nostrils flared, and a tight line of anger thinned his lips. "Damn you, Jordan. I'll show you interesting."

He buried his fingers in her hair, using it as an anchor to allow him easy access to her parted lips. His mouth was a weapon of warm, searing heat, conquering hers with a kiss that controlled and demanded and coerced.

"Nick, stop," she murmured, but her voice was devoid of conviction. When he took her mouth again in a longer, softer union, her lips parted of their own volition, eager to submit to his mastery. He left her mouth, unfulfilled, to trail a moist path to her ear. His breath sent tremors through her languid body.

"Stop," she moaned, "I can't play this game."

"Oh, lady," he sighed, "this is no game."

Some treacherous corner of her heart wanted to believe him. A sudden quickening filled her, tempt-ing her to let a light of hope into that small, dark corner. But another, stronger part remembered that this was his good-bye kiss: Soon he would leave her. Alone and hurting. She latched on to that thought with the tenacity of a woman hang-ing over the edge of a precipice.

"Nicholas," she said in the firmest tone she could muster with her body hammering that it, at least, was enjoying its sensual resurrection. "I don't want you to kiss me."

"You don't?" he asked, between kisses.

"N. . . no. I don't."

He stopped his restless nibbling and pulled back to

look at her with knowing eyes. "If I really believed that, Jordan, no matter how much I wanted you, I'd stop. And apologize for being a complete jerk."

"You don't need to apologize—"

"No, I don't. Because I don't believe you. Look me in the eye and tell me that you don't like it when I kiss you."

"I don't!" she answered, and felt the Pinocchio complex take hold. She was still weak from his kisses and aching for more.

"Liar."

"And how do you figure that, Mr. Estevis?"

"I don't figure it at all. I know it." He spoke with absolute certainty.

She started to argue, but his mouth swooped down to cover hers in a silencing kiss. Jordan felt as if every nerve in her body had been transported to her lips. She was aware of nothing but the feel of his mouth on hers.

"That's what you're going to get whenever you try to lie to me." His words were soft puffs of air as his mouth hovered near. "Consider it a lesson in honesty."

"I haven't lied to—" she started to protest, but he swallowed the rest of her words. His tongue stroked the inner edge of her parted lips, tasting her, inviting her to taste him; making her ache to taste him, to rediscover the contour and texture of him. Her nipples tautened in anticipation, and she felt a heated heaviness deep within her as she leaned into the kiss, pressed her body against his and felt his tantalizing maleness.

His kiss drugged her, left her with no thought processes, only wanting. Her hands moved restlessly. Up his arms, across his shoulders; until her fingers tangled in his thick raven hair. She urged him to explore her mouth and he obeyed willingly, drawing a moan of pleasure from her.

Nick shuddered with the force of his desire and tried to hold Jordan closer. But there was no space between them left unfilled, untouched. The ache in his loins grew more insistent, the need to touch her intimately too strong to deny.

He pulled his mouth from hers and sought the sweet curve of her neck. "So much fire," he whispered in a low, husky voice as his hand covered the swell of her breast. "So much fire you make me burn." Blind desire drove him, and he reached for the zipper of her flight suit, lowering it to her waist.

Jordan gasped as he cupped her naked breast, unaware of how much she wanted his touch until he gave it. Her senses spun, overwhelmed by the pleasure darting along her nerves. She pressed into his hand, wanting more, needing the feel of his mouth and his hands.

His hot, firm lips ground into hers, and she felt him shudder.

"God, I want you," he groaned. "Tell me what you want, Jordan. Tell me what you like."

She couldn't. She was too afraid of what her response might be.

"This?" he asked as his thumb moved slowly across the rigid tip of her nipple, sending waves of pulsing hunger shooting to the center of her womanhood. "Do you like this?"

Another tremor shook her when he nipped the sensitive skin of her neck with his teeth, then soothed the inflamed area with his lips and tongue.

Her pleasured moan lashed his need. He wanted to make love to her, right here, right now. With more strength than he knew he was capable of, he eased his hand from her breast, closing the opening of her suit with a fast, shaky jerk, not trusting himself to linger over the task. He wrapped her in his arms again, kissing her neck, her cheek, her brow, struggling to regain control. When he released her, he kept his eyes closed until his breathing slowed and the desire-tautened muscles in his body began to relax.

Jordan watched his iron will take command while she struggled just as hard with her own runaway emotions. Lord, how she wanted him. She felt as if the floodgates to every emotion she'd suppressed over the years had been opened wide. Her hunger for him was a raging flood, sweeping her barriers aside, drowning them in overpowering currents of desire.

"Oh, God," he whispered raggedly, dragging a shaking hand through his hair. He looked into her confused eyes. "I guess I got a little carried away." He smiled weakly. "But I'd do it again in a minute. I don't want to leave you." His face was soft with tenderness.

Her heart swelled.

"I don't think I'd better kiss you good-bye," he said with more than a hint of ruefulness. "I really need to leave, and if I touch you again . . ." He sighed, leaving the words unsaid.

But Jordan knew. And the knowing was almost as heady as if he had renewed his kisses. She gave him a tremulous smile of understanding.

"I'll call you just as soon as I have a chance." He reached toward her, but pulled back, knowing that even to touch her would be too much. He tilted his uplifted hand in a swift gesture of farewell and turned to leave, pausing after just a few steps for one last look.

"Take care of yourself, pretty lady." He smiled wolfishly. "I have some really interesting plans for our next meeting."

Jordan tunneled deeper under the covers certain the incessant pounding in her head was due to too many congratulatory toasts at Delia and Mark's surprise shower. If she could just pretend it was still dark outside, maybe she could fall back asleep and when she woke again, the pounding would be gone.

She let her thoughts wander to the night before. And all the nights before that. With Nick. He'd called every night since he'd left, giving her short descriptions of his days and long descriptions of what he'd rather be doing. With her. She'd missed his call last night. But she hadn't got home until after midnight, and had fallen asleep so quickly that she'd only had a few moments to think about him, to recreate their conversations and dwell on how her feelings for him were growing.

He was such an unconventional man. She'd thought the first flowers he'd sent her would also be the last, but he'd sent her two bouquets since he'd left. One for each week, with cards addressed "To My Favorite Pupil," and "For the Best-Looking Pilot I know." And there'd been three other cards. Funny little cards with comedic messages that bordered on the risqué. She loved them.

She smiled a lazy, sleepy smile, as visions of Nick warmed her, lulling her back to sleep. Almost. Her smile turned into a frown as the pounding started up again. Louder. Reluctantly, she eased the covers from over her head and forced her eyes open. She squinted into the sun-lightened room, letting her eyes adjust to the horrible shock of bright early daylight.

"Go away," she moaned. It was Saturday, for Pete's sake. And it couldn't be noon yet. She never got up before noon on . . .

Her eyes popped wide open. Saturday! Oh, murder! It was moving day! She must have overslept again, and Gary and Todd were pounding on the door to waken her.

"Just a minute!" she yelled at the top of her voice. She threw back the covers and grabbed her robe. "Don't go!" If she let them get away, she might never see them again. Though they'd offered to help, nobody liked going through the endless process of loading and unloading box after box after box. And Gary had warned her. Be up or else. The idea of trying to move without their help, and the pickup truck they'd promised, was enough to blast her out of bed like a rocket.

"I'm coming!" she shouted, bounding down the hall. She shoved a tangle of hair out of her eyes with one hand and opened the door with the other, bracing herself for Todd's never-ending grousing about people who slept away the best part of the day.

When she pulled the door open and saw who was standing there, she was struck with two simultaneous wishes. To fall through the floor and never be seen by man or beast again. Or to be blest with the speed of light so she could run to the bathroom, brush her teeth and hair, put on some makeup, and then come back and leap into his arms.

"Nick!" she croaked, taking in the low-slung jeans that hugged him like a long-lost friend. "What are you doing here?"

"Nothing, right at the moment." He gave her a dazzling smile. His gaze moved to the V of her satin robe. "But if you'd let me in, I could get real busy. Real quick." He visually caressed each curve outlined by the slinky fabric of her wrap and opened his arms, inviting her to make one of her wishes come partially true.

Without a second thought, she stepped into his embrace, relishing the sigh of contentment he breathed as his arms locked around her.

"You feel so good," his low voice rumbled, echoing her thoughts. "I didn't know I could miss somebody so much."

"When did you get back?" Her arms hugged him a little tighter at the reminder that they hadn't held him recently.

"Late last night." His lips moved down her neck to her shoulder in quick, scorching kisses. "I wanted to surprise you. And help you move." He pressed her closer against him. "I'm an excellent mover."

Oh, yes, indeed, Jordan agreed, as she felt every inch of his hard, muscular body. He showed all the signs of being a top-notch mover.

He trailed his kisses back along the path they had already taken, then foraged across her cheek, his parted lips ready to discover hers. She waited with breathless anticipation to feel his claiming touch, eager to surrender.

A broken chortle caused them to jump apart

like startled teenagers caught necking on the front porch.

"See, Gary. I told you she'd be up," Todd's voice intoned from the open front door.

Nick whirled around to face the two spectators standing just outside the entry. Jordan peeked around his massive shoulders to find Gary and Todd watching them with perplexed speculation.

"This is truly a day of miracles," Gary pronounced before Jordan could speak. "Not only is she up, but there is a man"— he nudged Todd for confirmation of the sighting—"in these hallowed grounds."

"There certainly is," Todd agreed, the inflection in his voice bringing an irate glance from Gary and a warning scowl from Nick.

Jordan laughed, knowing Todd enjoyed putting on airs. "Cut the act, Todd," she instructed. "This is Nick."

Todd pulled a frown. "Damn! And I was doing so well." His frown became a bit more delineated. "So," he said, giving Nick a hard look. "You're the one who's got our girl in such a dither."

Jordan felt herself blush all the way to her toes as Nick gave her a Cheshire smile. She hastily introduced her two blunt but well-meaning friends, and despite the uncertain look in Nick's eyes, excused herself to shower and change. When she returned to the living room, the three men were chatting amiably, and she knew a keen sense of relief that Nick had so easily accepted her friends, and they him.

"Well, guys," she said, rubbing her hands together in faked anticipation. "Are we all ready to get to work?"

Nick turned, and his smile froze on his face. His gaze pored over her cutoff jeans and the work shirt she'd tied up around her midriff.

"Ready?" Nick said, moving close enough so that only she could hear. "I'm ready, willing, and able." His eyes burned with a heated light. "And it would be anything but work."

Seven

Three hours and a lot of sweating later, Jordan surveyed the boxes scattered about her new apartment and heaved a sigh of relief. Since Nick had provided a company pickup, she and the three men had managed to move everything in just one trip. When he'd first seen her apartment, Nick had been amazed by her lack of possessions but she'd be willing to bet he was grateful now.

She walked across the hardwood floor of the living room to the remodeled kitchen and looked out the window to the street one floor below. She could see Gary and Todd walking back to the truck for another load of boxes. Nick's footsteps clattered up the flight of stairs that led to her door.

She was delighted that she'd be able to see up and down the old, treelined street as she stood at the kitchen window or sat on the small balcony outside her dining area. In fact, she was delighted with everything about her new apartment, from the claw-foot bathtub to the window-unit air conditioners. Everything in the converted house was a comfortable blend of old and new, and from the moment she'd seen it Jorden had loved it. The place answered her yearning for something solid and lasting in a world that seemed to move too fast, change too often.

A muscular arm slipped around her from behind, and warm breath teased her earlobe. A tangy, masculine scent drifted to her. She closed her eyes and leaned back into Nick's hard body. His free hand began to massage her thigh, just below the fringed edge of her cutoffs. The tips of his fingers grazed her skin in tingling patterns both soothing and exciting.

"Did I happen to mention that I love the way you look in cutoffs?" She could feel his words rumble beneath his chest. Wisps of her hair danced with his breath.

"I think," she said dreamily, "you might have mentioned it once or twice." She smiled to herself, remembering the way his gaze had roamed the length of her legs when he'd first seen her, the way he kept glancing at her throughout the morning. Sometimes he'd made a comment about how much he liked the way she looked, but more often his eyes told her in ways mere words couldn't express.

His fingers angled closer to the inner apex of her thigh, not quite daring to trespass the boundary of her clothing. The hand that had been holding her waist moved up the exposed skin of her stomach to the knotted ends of her blouse.

"And did I tell you how much I love this shirt?" Gentle waves of desire lapped at her, ebbing and flowing with each caress. Sunlight poured through the window, bathing her skin in a golden heat that matched her inner fire.

She almost moaned with grief when his hands slowly dropped away and he moved from behind her. She had to concentrate on remaining upright when he withdrew the support of his body.

The sound of Todd's laughter drifting up the stairwell told her why Nick pulled away, but it didn't ease her feeling of loss. The knowledge that she hadn't wanted him to stop touching her, that she would have let him continue, filled her with stunning certainty. Her breath caught as every protective instinct in her raced along shattered nerves. But those instincts were defenseless against other, deeper truths.

It had happened. Despite all her self-warning, despite the knowledge that she was opening herself to hurt far greater than any she had ever known, she loved him. Her chest tightened. She felt the sharp, cutting edge of pain. But it was too late. Even the aching prelude to what would surely come later couldn't change that. It was there. Beneath the heated desire, reaching up through the tangled web of old fears and new, love had pushed its way to the surface and blossomed.

A calming acceptance filled her as she turned to look at the man who had won her heart. The muscles in his back and arms bunched as he lifted a box marked *kitchen* onto the countertop. A lock of raven hair fell over his forehead. He opened the cardboard flaps of the box and peered inside before dipping his hand and withdrawing an aluminum pan. His gaze caught hers, and he winked.

Her heart somersaulted, and an answering smile parted her lips. She felt so . . . sure.

He must have read something in her eyes; Nick's gaze searched hers, and he carefully set the pan on the counter. He moved toward her, and she could see the question in his eyes, the hope. Did he want her love, she wondered, or just her surrender? But it didn't matter. It was too late for holding back. Too late for anything except loving him; for as long as he would let her.

His fingers whispered across her cheeks to tangle in her hair. His face filled her vision, allowing her heart to rediscover his eyes, his lips, the sculpted planes of his cheek, the slight stubble of hair that darkened his proud jaw. Everything about him took on new intensity, new beauty.

He studied her, too, before he drew closer and his mouth settled easily over hers. She felt as if she were weightless, a spirit floating toward the center of the universe. Her hands reached up to grasp his wrists, to feel the contact of something solid and real.

The thud of a heavy box hitting hardwood floor dimly penetrated her consciousness as Nick broke the kiss. His mouth left hers with a reluctance she understood and shared. He sighed and pressed his forehead to hers, his hands still holding her head. Slowly his fingers trailed from her hair, across her cheeks, and he pulled back to look into her eyes.

"Jordan?"

He didn't need to voice his question. He spoke with his eyes, his touch. And she answered with the same silent language. A language as old as time, as universal as love.

His expression turned quizzical. "Shall we go out to dinner tonight? Someplace special?"

A celebration, she thought. A prelude. Holding his gaze, she nodded, feeling her heart swell.

His features softened, his body relaxed, and she realized he hadn't been as certain of her answer as his manner implied. The knowledge that this confident, aggressive man was a little uncertain of her, a little vulnerable, tugged at the tender warmth in her heart. The hope she hadn't even realized she'd been nurturing soared. Could it be? Did he care for her more than she'd allowed herself to imagine? Had her own fears caused her to overlook or misread the extent of his feelings?

Stop it, she warned herself as Nick joined Gary and Todd in the living room and she began methodically placing dishes in cabinets. Her rational side tried to rein in the swirl of emotions, but they had broken free. Cherished dreams long denied, of love fulfilled, love returned, beckoned. And she gave in, telling herself it would cause no real harm. She knew no matter what direction her fantasies might take, reality was a far cry from wishful dreaming. She'd face reality later, when the dreams were not so vivid, not so new and unblemished.

How long she worked and dreamed, she didn't know. It seemed one minute she'd been standing with Nick, and the next minute the apartment was filled with a growing stack of empty boxes unpacked by Nick and Gary under Todd's capable direction.

She walked from room to room in stunned surprise. In the living area, Todd and Gary were arranging her small supply of books in built-in bookshelves. Her television had been set up in the small space between the shelves, directly across from the couch. The shower curtain was up in the bathroom, and towels and other linens had been stored in the proper closet. The box containing her personal items had been set just inside the door but left scrupulously untouched.

She ended her tour in the bedroom. Her heart almost stopped as she saw Nick, his back to her, making up her bed with militarily precise tucks. His movements grew languid as he directed his attention to the center of the bed, smoothing over the top sheet with slow, lingering passes. She had quick images of the bed, sheets kicked back in abandon, Nick's hands floating over her skin with the same careful attention he was now giving the sheets.

He reached for the blue satin comforter, turning his head so she had a view of his face. Her breath caught at the unmistakable desire that tautened his features. A ragged sigh hissed through his parted lips just before he noticed her. The swift surge of emotions playing across his face fascinated her. Surprise eclipsed desire, muting to delight. Delight became hopeful speculation, ending in a rueful smile.

"Just daydreaming," he explained. His eyes lighted with wicked mischief. "Care to test my handiwork? I've been told I have an excellent technique with beds."

A familiar green-eyed nymph taunted her. "Oh, really?"

"By my top sergeant, of course," he hastened to add. Devilment gleamed behind his sooty lashes, belying the serious mask of his face.

"Of course," Jordan said, her expression equally grave.

"You don't believe me? Look at it." Her gaze followed his to the bed, and again images superimposed themselves. Her breath caught.

His voice lowered, as if he shared her vision. "See how smooth the sheets are?" The twinkle in his eye flared to an ember, drawing her to him with the magical pull of unspoken delight. He cupped her face in his hand, stroking the skin of her cheek with calculated slowness. "Smooth and soft." Only a fool would have thought he meant the sheets.

Muffled laughter drifted from the kitchen, a worrisome interruption they chose to ignore. Nick looked away from her, back down at the bed, and her gaze followed. His strong, tanned hand moved to the pillowcase, gliding and swirling over the white lace in mesmerizing caresses.

He moved, imperceptibly, yet so near, his chest was only a breath away from hers. Then he inhaled, brushing against her with a featherlike touch. The tips of her breasts tingled as they tightened and peaked, straining to maintain the light contact.

"Such soft perfection," Nick breathed, closing his eyes against the exquisite pleasure of her response. He swelled and hardened, wanting her, loving the way she wanted him.

He touched her neck, and Jordan sighed, absorbing his warmth, the sensual feel of his caress. But her gaze remained locked on the bed, on the silky white blur of delicate fabric clinging to padded strength.

Nick's hands moved with slow deliberation, gliding over her shoulders, down her arms, allowing his thumbs to trace along the outer edge of her breasts, tantalizing her with the fleeting caress. Each touch was light, perfect, stirring her until desire flowed like warm, sweet honey. He continued his journey along her body, charting the indentation of her waist to the flare of her hips and settling there, with his thumbs bordering the valley of her femininity. She knew he was watching her, watching her gaze travel down the bed as his hands traveled down her body.

"So tight," he murmured, when her gaze rested on the perfect tucks of the sheet. "Sheathing and anchoring." His thumbs moved erotically closer to her aching center. "Holding with silken strength." He cupped her buttocks and lifted her against himself. "Just the way it should be. The way it will always be, when I make your bed."

Jordan's gaze followed her heart, and sought the rugged face so close to hers. His eyes were closed, the half-moon of his thick lashes casting a light shadow over his cheeks. She wanted to tell him how much she loved him, but caution held her tongue. What if the feelings weren't mutual? What if it spoiled the beauty, the magic, of the moment?

He sighed and tried to smile, but it was no use. He felt clammy, sticky with sweat that had nothing to do with room temperature. He wanted her so badly he was hurting, almost sick with the need to bury himself deep inside her. He was throbbing, pulsing with hunger.

"Oh Jordan," he breathed. "That was an idiotic thing to do." His eyes opened; bright, burning embers. "It's taking every ounce of control I can muster not to throw you on the bed and undo all my hard work."

He shook his head with resigned acceptance when footsteps echoed from the living room. "Why is it that we're never alone?"

"I thought we were," she whispered, unable to control the thready quality of her voice.

He considered her words. "We were, weren't we? That's what's so special about us. Every time we meet, every time we touch, nothing exists but the two of us." He smiled softly, then held her until his body relaxed. "Right now, I guess we'd better try to remember Todd and Gary. And lunch."

"Lunch?" she asked vaguely, not quite ready to let go of their intimacy.

He looked wicked again. "Yeah, lunch. Expending so much energy on a bed always makes me hungry."

She pursed her lips in exasperation. "You're asking for it, Nicholas."

He gave a contented sigh. "I'm so glad you noticed."

Nick pulled his car to a smooth stop in front of Jordan's apartment and killed the engine. Neither had spoken during the short drive from the intimate supper club, content to let interlocked fingers and long kisses at stoplights speak for them. Each kiss had become stronger, more intense, as the glare of downtown Phoenix faded to the occasional streetlight of the residential areas. His gentle squeezing of her hand and the rhythmic strumming of his thumb over hers was an erotic message to her heightened senses.

Wrapped in a velvet cloak of desire, Jordan felt

her body grow warmer as Nick opened the door and slid out of the car. Even his most casual movements had a controlled power behind them. The muscles in his thighs rippled beneath his slacks as he walked around the front of the low silver Porsche. Every step was smooth, assertive, powerful.

He helped her from the car and hugged her to his side, pressing the length of their bodies together. The walk from his car to her apartment was just as silent as the ride had been, just as full of charged electricity. Though there was no hand-holding, no stolen kisses, Jordan sensed a new tension in Nick as they walked to her apartment; a dormant energy held tightly in check.

She scarcely had time to lock the apartment door before he pulled her into his arms, his mouth covering hers in hungry urgency. She wrapped her arms around his lean waist, clutching at him, so empty and aching that she moaned in relief when his tongue filled the hollow of her mouth.

She couldn't get close enough, couldn't touch him enough, feel him the way her body craved. All evening long she'd thought of this, wanted this. She lifted his jacket and splayed her hands over his back. But it still wasn't enough. She needed to feel his skin under her hands, to trace the corded muscles that were so easily defined under the thin covering of his shirt. She worked the soft fabric from the band of his slacks and slid her hands beneath it, gasping in satisfaction. He felt like warm satin as her fingers explored his naked flesh with frantic delight, clinging to his shoulders before sliding down to the trim flesh of his waist.

Her response was nearly Nick's undoing, threatening to unleash the tight rein he'd held on himself all evening. But somehow he knew he had to take it slowly, make it last.

"Jordan, Jordan." Her name became a litany he chanted in the brief moments he could tear his mouth away from the heady delight of hers. "I want you so," he breathed against her lips just seconds before he took them again.

His hand moved to her breast, and she gasped, unprepared for the scorching pleasure of his touch, the wild fury of her response.

"Tell me," he ordered, power and passion in his voice. "Tell me what you want."

"I want you," she heard herself say, as hungry need fired her words. "I've never wanted the way I want you."

He stared at her with stormy eyes. For a breathless moment she feared she'd said something wrong, or said too much. But then she saw the turbulence clear, the corners of his mouth lift in an attempted smile.

"You have me," he whispered, lifting her into his arms, holding her high against his chest. "You have me."

She pressed her face into his neck, breathing in his masculinity, absorbing his passion. He carried her through the apartment into her darkened bedroom. The light from the hall illuminated a golden path to her bed, and he stopped there, slipping his arm from under her knees, lowering her to her feet.

She ran her trembling hands along the solid wall of his chest to the knot of his tie. She wanted to take off his clothing and feel the velvet heat of his skin, to run her hands over the mat of hair on his chest, and to define the contours of his muscles with her fingertips. Her need made her weak, her fingers clumsy, as she worked in a useless attempt to loosen his tie.

"Let me," he murmured.

His hands covered hers and guided them to a resting place on his chest. He slipped the tie from around his neck, but she couldn't be still, and restlessly worked the buttons of his shirt. As soon as she'd opened a path, she dipped her fingers under the fabric and caressed the muscled swell, brushing her fingertips over his hardened nipples.

He gasped his pleasure at her touch; a shudder racked his body. He attacked the remaining buttons with his own hands, shrugging out of his shirt and jacket in one frenzied motion. His movements thrust his chest closer to her hungry mouth, and she took advantage of the offering, planting adoring kisses along the ridge of his breast.

"Oh, God," he groaned. Her mouth was like a flame, licking at his passion, driving his desire higher. "Do you know how that feels?"

"Show me, Nick," she pleaded huskily, "show me."

Immediately his arms were around her, hands unzipping her dress, pulling it off her shoulders. She clung to the rippling muscles in his arms as he pushed the dress down around her waist and hips, letting it fall to the floor in a soft whisper of silk. Only the peach lace of her teddy covered her breasts, her nipples clearly visible through the gossamer strands.

His hands spanned her waist, massaging the sleek satin against her skin in fevered caresses before moving upward. As his thumbs neared her breasts, her heart began to pound, thundering its excitement when he cupped her fullness, weighing and measuring each breast, stroking the sensitive buds through fragile lace.

An insidious weakness crept through her as she reveled in the erotic pleasure of his touch, exploding with fierce, uncontrolled need. She grabbed his forearms to steady herself.

Nick's heart fell to his stomach when he felt her panicked touch. He sought her eyes, praying he wouldn't see regret.

"What's wrong?" he whispered.

"My knees are shaking," she answered in a soft, passion-filled voice.

Relief made him weak. "So are mine," he admitted, pressing his forehead against hers in an effort to slow the momentum of his passion. He took a deep, shuddering breath, but it was too late. His hands moved in a dreamlike motion and peeled the chemise down over the swell of her breasts and hips. She kicked off her shoes as the bit of lace fell to the floor. He imagined it skimming over her bare legs, pooling at her feet, but clinging to his last vestige of control, he didn't allow himself to watch the sensuous unveiling.

Jordan looked up into black, fiery depths. He held her gaze, and she read in his eyes that she was beautiful to him, that he didn't need to see her nakedness to know she would please him. Then he stepped back, lowering his gaze in a slow, exploring descent that seared her wherever it lingered.

He swallowed, hard, parted his lips as if to speak only to emit a ragged sigh. She would have laughed at his sudden failure of speech if it hadn't been for the exquisite torture of his face. His eyes were blazing, his face hard with skin stretched taut over high cheekbones.

He gathered her into his arms, pressing her tightly to him. Her breasts burned into his chest. Her hair smelled of herbs and sunshine, and he buried his face in the silken strands, wanting to absorb the scent of her. She was soft and simmering, and he couldn't wait any longer. He placed a knee on the mattress, using it to balance their weight as he slowly lowered her to the bed.

He looked down at her, watching the rise and fall of her breasts, watching them respond to his bold caresses before lowering his head, taking an aching tip into his mouth. She'd never felt such ecstasy as the wet heat of his suckling mouth, the swirl of his flickering tongue. Her fingers tangled in his hair and she pressed him closer, offering more of herself, urging him to take her.

She reached for him, craving the comfort of his solid weight. Her hand found his bare chest, and she satisfied her need to touch him there, then she angled her hand downward, following the coarse tendrils of hair as they tapered to a thin line leading directly to the object of her desire. Her need to know his strength was thwarted as her hand encountered the leather of his belt. Her fingers worked frantically on the buckle, but before she could complete her task, Nick pulled away from her and heaved himself from the bed.

He was naked before she lost the urgency, the intense need that consumed her like wildfire. Her breath caught when she saw his naked beauty, intensifying the torrent of sensations inside her.

He was masculine perfection, strong, powerful; each muscle hard and unyielding under smooth bronzed skin.

She held out her arms, eager to touch him, to praise him with her hands, to tell him with her body what she was afraid to speak out loud. That she loved him; loved him with an intensity that frightened her.

He came to her, lowering himself over her. The muscles in his arms bulged as he held his weight above her, brushing back and forth over her breasts, teasing her nipples with his hair-roughened chest. She wrapped her arms around him, trying to pull him closer, aching to feel him inside her.

He shifted his weight, balancing on one elbow, reaching blindly to trail his fingers over and between her breasts while he watched her face, dark passion thundering in his eyes. His hand moved from her breasts to her stomach, lower, circling the aching center of her need.

He captured her moan, his tongue thrusting into her mouth at the same instant his fingers discovered the source of her fire. Soft, rythmic, smooth. He stroked her, teased her, knowing instinctively how to touch her, how to please her. Her whole being centered on the consuming pleasure he brought her as her senses spun wildly.

He moved between her thighs, pressing his strength against her, probing, teasing, but holding back until she was arching against him, straining to make him come to her, to assuage her driving hunger.

"Tell me," she heard him whisper raggedly, and opened her eyes to see the strain in his face, the price he was paying to hold back his own fulfillment. "Tell me."

"I want you," she murmured through the haze of her passion. "I want you now. Now."

Her words ended in a gasp as he entered her, filling her with his thick, velvety length. She met his powerful thrust, urging him deeper, wanting all of the strong, vital core of him within her.

Her fingers tangled in his hair, and she pulled his mouth to hers. She knew the masculine scent of him, the sweet, demanding taste of him, heard him whisper how she pleased him, how he wanted her, needed her. His movements grew more forceful. Thrusting, plunging deeper and deeper, drawing the tension tighter around her, urging her to reach, to plead for release.

Their mouths touched again and again as their bodies met, filling her with a wildness she hadn't known she was capable of, a beauty she'd never known before; filling her until the beauty soared, exploded, bursting through her in rippling shock waves at the exact moment she heard him gasp, felt him shudder his own release.

She lay in his arms, resting beside him in luxurious contentment, certain she'd never known anything as wonderful, as complete, as loving him. Nothing had ever made her feel so whole and alive, even at the moment when her body was most out of control, her senses spiraling toward some hitherto-unknown region of delight.

Nick stirred, rolling to his side to balance on one elbow as he smoothed her sweat-dampened hair from her face. She opened her eyes to the wonder of his gaze.

"I knew we'd be good together," he said, his

voice still husky. "But I never dreamed it could be like this." He closed his eyes and shook his head. "Never like this."

Her chest ached with the love she felt for him as she watched him grapple with his own unexpected discovery.

"There is one problem, however," he said, drawing his brows together.

Her heart stopped beating. "A problem?"

"Just a slight one, at the moment." He lowered his mouth to hers, and she closed her eyes as delight shimmered through her again. "But it's getting bigger by the second."

He pressed against her, and she felt the evidence of his renewed arousal.

"I can't seem to get enough of you," he said in a low, rough voice.

And then he made love to her again. Taking her slowly to peak after peak. Touching. Tasting. Pleasuring. Until her senses exploded with wild, sweet madness and she was melting into him, soaring into the splendor of shattering release.

Eight

Her eyes adjusted slowly to the dimly lit room, and Jordan stirred beneath the unfamiliar weight of Nick's arm curved under her breasts. She could tell by his deep, even breathing that he was sleeping, that whatever had awoken her hadn't disturbed him. She turned her head cautiously, not wanting to wake him, but curious to see him, knowing full well that only children looked precious and heart-wrenchingly beautiful when they slept. Men and women only looked . . . slack. Slack-jawed, slack-bodied. Limp. Crumpled.

Wrong. Sleek was the word that described Nick. Sleek and hard and infinitely, beautifully masculine. He lay on his stomach, one arm stretched over his pillow, the other thrown possessively across her. The light from the hallway etched him in a golden glow, painting shadow pictures across the dips and hollows of his firm musculature. A sharp sensation danced through her chest, pain and joy intertwined.

"Why are you awake?"

His voice was soft, still lazy with sleep, but it shouted through the protective darkness, making her start.

"What is it?" The sheets rustled and the mattress gave under his weight as he moved closer.

"Nothing," she said, wondering why she had to force the word. "What could possibly be wrong?" The question was meant for herself as much as for him.

"No second thoughts?" he asked, pulling her into the curve of his naked body. "No regrets?"

She shook her head in denial. "Of course not." She twined her leg around his and rubbed up and down the sinewy, hair-roughened surface. How could she regret giving him her love? "It's just been a long time since I've shared a bed with anyone."

He stroked her hair with a slow, gentle hand. "I don't want you to feel uncomfortable with me. Ever."

"It's not that I'm uncomfortable . . . exactly."

Nick's heart thudded with a dull, aching burn. Disappointment weighted him like a shroud. He'd thought tonight had meant her acceptance, her commitment. He'd known—at least he'd thought he'd known—inviting him into her bed was synonomous with inviting him into her life. He'd been wrong. Again.

"Do you want me to go?" The words stung as much as his thoughts.

"No," she answered almost before he finished asking. No, she didn't want him to go. And that, she realized was the source of her unease. She didn't want him to go. Not tonight. Not tomorrow.

Not ever. But he would—someday. That was the inevitable, the one true given. Sooner or later, he'd leave her. Only love would make him stay beyond the passion, and not once during their glorious lovemaking, not once in his whispered words of pleasure, had he so much as hinted that his feelings went beyond raw desire. And useless as it was, it hurt. She'd known from the beginning it would be this way. But still . . . it hurt.

"Where are we going?" Jordan asked for at least the twelfth time. She turned sideways so she could have a better view of Nick, and hooked her arm over the back of the burgundy leather seat. Even after a week of being with him almost constantly, of being his lover and knowing each centimeter of him with complete intimacy, she still couldn't look at him enough.

He glanced away from the road long enough to throw her a wicked grin.

"Let's just say it has something to do with breakfast."

"We've already had breakfast," she reminded him.

"And a superb one it was." He shot her another look, one full of a different, much more intimate pleasure. "From the first course to the very exquisite dessert." His gaze traveled boldly from her breasts to the cradle of her thighs. "Just the kind of breakfast in bed every man should have at least once a day."

"It does have certain advantages over sitting on the floor," she agreed, remembering the fun they'd had sharing Frosted Flakes and Rice Krispies, sneaking spoonfuls from each other's bowls as they sat cross-legged in the center of her bed. She smiled as she remembered how Nick had teased her for pulling the sheet up over their laps. He didn't mind having a little milk slopped on him if she didn't, he'd assured her. And then he'd deliberately drizzled the cold white liquid over her breasts and washed it away with his mouth.

"Quit smiling like that," he ordered. "You'll make me forget where I'm going."

"And where might that be?"

He just chuckled and trained his eyes on the road. She took the opportunity to do what she loved best, watch him. Before Nick, she hadn't really been aware of just how much a man expressed his personality through his body, the way he moved and cared for it. Nick was clean, concise, aggressive, sensual. Just like his body. Just like his walk, the way he used his hands, thrust out his chin . . . made love.

She watched the muscles in his thigh tighten beneath the denim of his faded jeans as he shifted gears and maneuvered the car around a sharp turn. Power. So much to learn, so much to know. Would she have enough time? she wondered in a sudden surge of panic. Would she ever see all the layers of the inner man? Would she ever uncover his heart?

Stop it! she warned herself as she did each time her thoughts veered in that direction. A week of loving, a week of wondering, wouldn't change a thing, hadn't changed a thing. He wanted her, enjoyed her, cared for her. But that didn't mean love. She'd had to bite back her own confession so many times she wondered how he couldn't sense it, couldn't see it pouring from her eyes, feel it in her touch. But she'd never said the words, never would, unless he spoke them first. She had to hold back that much, her pride demanded it. She'd given him everything else.

Another sharp turn pulled her out of her heavy thoughts. The car's engine slowed to a purr, and she realized they were coasting to a stop in a parking lot. An antique furniture dealer's parking lot.

"What are we doing here?" If Nick had a weakness for antiques, he hadn't mentioned it before.

"Finding you a table."

"Here?" Her voice squeaked. She couldn't afford any costly antiques right now, not after paying the agency fee, security deposit and advance rent on her new apartment.

He walked around the front of the Porsche and opened her door. "Since you like antiques, I thought you might enjoy looking here."

"My furniture isn't antique," she said with a strained laugh. "It's just old."

"Well, so is this stuff."

"Nick—" She started to tell him no, that it was silly to look before she could afford to buy. But he looked so pleased with his surprise. "This is great!" she said, trying to sound enthused. It couldn't hurt to just look, she told herself, letting him help her from the car.

Five minutes later she was unshakably, irreversibly in love. With a drop-leaf table and four ladder-back, cane-bottom chairs.

"Yes, it's lovely," she assured the dealer, running her fingertips over the patinaed table surface. She could see the glow of victory in the salesman's eyes. He was no fool. He knew lust when he saw it.

"When can you deliver it?" Nick asked, throwing her into another panic.

"No!" she yelped.

The dealer studied her over flaring nostrils, as if she'd just been sick all over his best Persian rug.

"You don't like it?" Nick asked, confused.

"Of course I like it!" she assured them both. "I love it; I just can't buy it."

"Of course you can't," Nick told her, speaking like an adult telling a child why spinach is good for him. "I'm buying it."

"You want the table?"

"No. *You* want the table. Don't you?"

Awareness dawned. "You are *not* buying that table for me."

"Well, I'm not buying it for my brother."

"Nicholas"—Jordan used her most intimidating glare—"I will not allow you to buy me that table."

"You moved out of a perfectly good apartment where you could use a perfectly good set of bar stools because of KJTX." He glowered. "I own KJTX. Therefore, I am responsible for your move and for your not having a place to sit down and eat and I *will* buy you that table."

"No."

Nick sighed heavily and closed his eyes, clearly fighting amused frustration. He opened his eyes and smiled at her, an unnervingly sweet smile, then turned to the proprietor.

"May we use your office for just one moment?"

Nodding, the proprietor waved a stubby hand toward a heavy wooden door marked PRIVATE.

Jordan followed Nick into the enclosed area and waited for the attack, pride swelling. Right was on her side. He could get as arrogant as he liked, use all the logic in the world. It wouldn't change a thing. She could not accept such an expensive gift. She was not . . .

Coming from the tiny office, Jordan knew her lips were still swollen from Nick's ardent kisses, and her face flushed even redder when the dealer shot her a knowing glance after assuring Nick that the table would be delivered Monday evening.

"You drive a hard bargain, lady," Nick murmured as he escorted her still-wobbly body out the door.

"And you fight dirty."

"I fight to win," he said, and shrugged. "I don't usually give nearly as many concessions as you managed to get today."

"I'd hardly call coercing me into letting you pay half the cost of my table a concession." A tingle danced through her as she relived the persuasive caress that had won him that point.

He opened the car door, placing himself between her and the frame, one arm resting on the roof, the other draped over the door. "But I wanted to buy it for you," he said. "As a gift. Haven't you ever heard the old adage about accepting gifts gracefully?"

"I've also heard about being wary of Greeks bearing gifts."

He gave her an innocent look. "I just wanted to buy you a present."

She couldn't resist stepping into his arms. "I know that. You were just being you. A wonderfully generous man." She nipped at his lips with penitent kisses. "I'm an ungrateful witch."

"Does this mean I get my way?" he murmured into her hair.

"No," she sighed, feigning remorse. "This means you get to try and do a little more convincing."

Spotless white table cloth, candlelight, centerpiece, and soft . . . music! She'd forgotten the music! Jordan hurried to the bedroom and grabbed the clock radio, yanking the cord from the wall socket. She plugged it into a kitchen outlet and switched the stations until she found slow, easy-listening music—not her usual choice, but somehow tonight called for something a little more sensual than country rock.

She glanced at the time and felt her heart zoom. Nine-twenty. Nick would be here any minute. She ran her hands down her ivory silk tunic and checked to make sure the ankle ties of her harem pants were secure.

· Well, she was ready. Her only remaining concern was dinner. Please, God, she prayed, let Sally's recipe be as foolproof as she promised. Jordan Donner in the kitchen was a joke. Only Sally's assurances that even her twelve-year-old could roast a chicken without endangering the taste buds of the entire family had convinced Jordan to try to prepare a romantic, home-cooked meal. If only Nick weren't cutting down on red meat, she thought. She'd feel much more confident with a thick, juicy steak.

Her stomach growled, reminding her that nine-thirty was an obscene hour to be having dinner. Nick was probably either starved or had already cheated and nibbled something at home. But what could she do? She'd had to cover the jackknifed eighteen-wheeler. Live meant live. And then she'd had to postflight and log out and confer with the news producer. Since she was on call tonight, she was supposed to have tomorrow off and she'd wanted to make sure there had been no change in her schedule. She anticipated a late night. She just wished . . . no, she didn't wish she had normal working hours. She'd chosen this field to make her mark, to prove that she was more than just another pretty face, another spoiled rich girl. She could do it, too. She had to. If only proving herself didn't mean odd hours.

She heard footsteps on the stairs, and her heart started its usual jitterbug whenever she knew Nick was near. She took a deep, calming breath before going to the door.

Why was it, she wondered as her gaze swept over his face, that she could never get used to seeing him standing there? That every time she saw him she started tingling?

"Don't I get to come in?"

His question pulled her thoughts from the fit of his ice-blue polo shirt and dove-gray slacks to the knowing amusement dancing in his eyes.

"Only if you promise to be on your best behavior," she said, unable to disguise the sudden huskiness in her voice.

"I'm always good with you." He didn't even try to hide the less than innocent meaning behind his words.

She couldn't argue with that, she thought, stepping aside to let him enter. He waited until she closed the door before he drew her into his arms.

"You look beautiful tonight," he said after a

lingering "hello" kiss. "But then you always look beautiful. Even in those godawful flight suits."

She pulled a frown. "My flight suits aren't awful. They're meant to be functional, not sexy."

"Well, they are that. Functional, I mean." He smiled wickedly. "Those zippers function just great."

Jordan shot him a warning glance, though she felt her body temperature rise a notch at the memory of Nick's strong fingers sliding the metal fastener of her flight suit down, reaching inside and . . .

The timer on the oven screeched the announcement that dinner was ready, pulling her thoughts from the exciting to the mundane.

"I'd be willing to settle for a late supper," Nick said with seductive laziness, holding her a little tighter when she tried to move out of the circle of his arms.

"This *is* a late supper," she reminded him. Pushing away from his inviting prison, she walked to the kitchen to turn off the timer. When she opened the oven, a blast of hot air peppered her face with the tantalizing aroma of wine and herbs. The bird within looked like every woman's Thanksgiving dream: plump, nicely browned, simmering in the aromatic sauce she'd used for basting. Perfect.

She used hot pads to pull the roasting pan from the oven, feeling a thrill of pride that she had actually produced something that looked and smelled so luscious.

"Oh, Nick! Look!" She couldn't keep the wonder out of her tone. "I did it!"

She glanced up from the chicken long enough to see the questioning look in his eyes.

"This is my first roast chicken," she explained with pride, then admitted sheepishly, "I'm not much for cooking."

He took the bird, which she'd put on a serving platter, and carried it to the table while she got the salad from the refrigerator and set a bowl of scalloped potatoes, Betty Crocker style, on the table.

"You didn't need to go to all this trouble, sweetheart. We could have gone out."

Her heart trembled at his casual endearment. Sweetheart. How precious it was to her. Could he ever, in his wildest dreams, imagine what that one little word meant to her? He might not have meant it as any more than a casual nickname, nothing more than all the darlings and sweetie babies and a million other insincere throwaways she'd heard in her lifetime. But for her it was different. It made her special to him, and that was all that mattered.

"I wanted to do it for you. I wanted to spend our last evening together completely alone." The spoken reminder that he would be gone for over a week dampened her spirits. But she forced a smile and motioned toward the carving set she'd purchased especially for tonight. "Now, if you'll do the honors while I serve the salad?"

He returned her smile and picked up the utensils. "This is going to be great," he said, stabbing the fork into the chicken breast and working the knife across a leg joint. Jordan watched, waiting with pleased anticipation for the meat to "fall off the bone" as Sally had promised. But it didn't. A foreboding shadow loomed on her horizon. She'd followed Sally's directions exactly. What could be wrong?

Nick's cutting motions grew just a little firmer, and she saw the leg separate from the body, clinging with tenacious strings of meat that Nick neatly severed with the knife. She breathed a sigh of relief when the second leg was cut free and the breast sliced into firm, if rather ragged, pieces. The meat was nice and white, as Sally had told her it would be, a sure sign it was cooked thoroughly.

Nick helped himself to a leg and breast piece, while Jordan took only a serving of white meat. She tried not to look too obvious, too eager to hear his praise, but she couldn't hide her smile of satisfaction when Nick picked up the leg. She watched eagerly as he sank his perfect white teeth into the fleshy drumstick.

He bit into the meat with obvious relish—then froze. His eyes widened slightly, and he shifted in his chair, his teeth still sunken into the golden-brown leg. Time stood still. She watched him wrestle with the cooked fowl until, at last, he pulled free. Her gaze zeroed in on the stringy slivers of meat dangling from the drumstick as Nick placed it back on his plate. Her mind held that picture as she glanced up to his face and watched him chew. And chew. And chew. He was trying, she knew, to keep his expression neutral. But it was hopeless. Nick was no actor.

She took a hesitant bite of her own serving and nearly choked on the dry particles that stuck to her tongue like chunks of concrete. Nothing could force her throat to open, her jaw muscles to work. She grabbed her glass of chilled Chablis and tried to drown the tenacious clumps.

"It's awful," she gasped, when at last she could speak. She looked to Nick for confirmation.

"A little chewy," he said. "But the flavor is . . . unique. Did you say this was chicken?"

"Yes, it's chicken!" she snapped, throwing her napkin down as she sprang from her chair and grabbed the serving plate. "Plain old everyday chicken!" Waves of frustrated anger pounded through her as she dumped the bird into the trash. "A perfectly good hen. A regular piece of meat until I got hold of it. Leave it to me to take the plumpest, best-looking stewing hen in the whole town of Phoenix and turn it into roast leather."

"Stewing hen?"

His surprised tone silenced her. She turned to face him before he could completely mask the amusement in his expression.

"You baked a stewing hen?"

"A chicken is a chicken, Nick!" Her voice sounded strained even to her own ears. She knew if she didn't calm down, she would dissolve into a heap of self-pity. Damn! She'd tried so hard to impress him.

His muffled laughter didn't do a thing to help her battered ego. "Honey—" His voice broke suspiciously. "Even I know that stewing hens are too old to be roasted. They're for . . . stewing."

"But—" She remembered how long she'd stood in the poultry section at the store and agonized over which bird to pick. She hadn't wanted to get one too small or one too big. And then she'd seen the little separate section of whole chickens marked stewing hens; they'd been closer to the size she was looking for. The other section was labeled fryers, and it had made more sense to her to buy a stewer. Fryers were for frying. Stewers were for not frying. Or so she'd assumed.

She tried to smile at him. She really did. But she felt like such a fool. She knew next to nothing about cooking. Her mother had always warned her never to bother the cook. And when she'd been married to Clark, they too had had a live-in housekeeper who did all the cooking. As a single woman, she'd learned the basic survival skills but she was no chef. And now she'd made a fiasco out of dinner. Her quavering smile broke and, to her dismay, she felt tears threaten again.

"Oh, Jordan." Nick's voice was low with concern as he left the table and moved to take her in his arms. "You're not going to cry are you? Not over something like this?"

He nestled her against his solid warmth, stroking her hair, kissing the top of her head.

His tenderness opened the floodgates. "I wanted it to be perfect," she moaned between sobs. "I wanted it to be wonderful, so you'd think I was wonderful and—"

"I already know how wonderful you are." He soothed, rocking her slowly, wanting to give her the same comfort her confession had given him. She was opening up to him, letting him in at last. "Don't you know how special you are to me? How good I feel just being with you?" He tilted her face toward him. "You make me remember I wasn't born just to work; that I can relax and enjoy life, that I can laugh. I love being with you." His lips feathered across her cheek. "You give me things I never knew I wanted and make me want things I'd forgotten existed. How could anyone be more special than that?"

He stroked and petted her until the rhythmic movements of his body made a subtle change, so smooth, so gradual, that at first she was unaware comfort had been replaced by something less soothing, less peaceful.

"You're perfect, Jordan," he whispered as his lips hovered near her ear. "Warm, intelligent, beautiful."

"I—" She shivered as his mouth worked its magic. And she pressed her body closer to his. "I can't cook."

"It doesn't matter," he murmured. "I can. Or we'll eat out."

His hands moved over her, cupping her hips and lifting her so that his hardness was pressed against the soft mound between her thighs.

"No one can make me feel the way you do." His voice was husky. His hands skimmed up her back, taking the soft fabric of her silk blouse with them. He didn't stop until he pulled it free, exposing her lace-covered breasts to his burning gaze. The silk drifted to an unnoticed heap on the floor as he worked the front clasp of her bra, parting the gossamer weave with slow, deliberate hands.

"You respond so perfectly." He drew his thumb across her breast, and her nipple got tighter. "That's all I need, Jordan. Just you, wanting me."

Her senses spun wildly, his words as thrilling as his touch. So much, he made her feel so much, want so much more.

He bent his knees, lowering his face to her breasts. His arms encircled her waist as his mouth closed hotly over her nipple, pulling waves of pulsing need through her feverish body.

Her head dropped back as she thrust out her breasts in offering. The swirling torrents of her passion rose higher, and she couldn't stop the moan of pleasure that broke from her throat. She loved him, wanted him, needed to bind him to her in the only way she could. She caught his hair in her hands, wanting his lips on hers, wanting to pull his tongue into her mouth in the same way she wanted to pull his body into hers.

But he wouldn't be hastened by her feverish urgings. His tongue laved her breast in moist heat, and he teased it to an even tighter peak. His teeth nipped with tender pain, flooding her with deeper hunger. One arm tightened about her waist, while the other settled beneath the curve of her buttocks, and suddenly he lifted her, carrying her with powerful ease.

He took her into the living room and lowered her to the couch. His husky breathing filled her ears, and an unexpected surge of elation filled her soul. For the first time she realized that it was she, not what she did or how she did it, but merely she, that excited him. She was enough, in and of herself.

She reached up to take off his shirt, eager to share the heady delight of her newfound confidence, but her hands met only air. Gently he removed her sandals and loosened the ankle ties of her pants. In seconds she lay naked except for the sheer triangle of satin that curved over her hips.

Next he removed his own clothes. The taut muscles of his stomach flexed as he lifted his shirt over his head. She could almost feel the velvety texture of his bare skin, the heat and steel that rippled beneath.

Then his lips touched her ankle, her calf, the bend of her knee. His fingers rolled the silken barrier from her hips and his breath, hot and ragged, braised her thigh as he parted her legs. The flicker of his tongue unleashed starbursts of heat that shimmered through her veins in a rush of molten pleasure. She was incapable of thought, unable to hide behind the curtain of natural reserve. She could only feel, only gasp and tremble with each successive spasm of delight. Her fingers twined in his hair, an anchor to hold her within the realms of earth as wave after wave of sensation lifted her higher.

Suddenly he moved, filling her with his hot, powerful length. Her legs wrapped around his hips, her arms around his shoulders, and she arched into him, meeting his driving thrusts again and again until she felt the shock waves of explosive release. And still he drove into her, gasping her name as his body grew rigid and he met his own sweet shattering.

She clung to him as he relaxed, pulling his head to her shoulder and relishing the hot, slick weight of his body.

"How can I leave you?" he whispered, echoing her own thoughts. "I'm addicted to you." He shifted onto one elbow and drew his hand across her stomach. "Mm, your skin is so soft. I can't imagine anything smoother than this." His hand skimmed over her breasts, up to her face, where his fingertips feathered across her cheek. He dipped his head and kissed her parted lips. "I love the taste of you," he whispered softly, making her heart skitter over the words.

Love me! she wanted to shout. Me! But for the one thing she wanted most in this world, she couldn't ask. Nick was no bashful boy, no inarticulate suitor too shy to speak his feelings. If he loved her, he would tell her in the same bold way he proclaimed his desire. That he said nothing was confession enough. Her chest heaved with the process of accepting.

"Let's go to bed." He smiled down at her, his mouth soft, his eyes tinged with the faintest hint of bemusement. "I want to stay here tonight, to hold you all night long." He spoke with slow hesitancy, as if the words, the thoughts behind the words, were foreign to him. "I need to feel you beside me when I fall asleep, and when I wake up, I want to kiss the sleep from your eyes and make love to you again."

She let the sweetness wash over her, fill her with hopeless joy. She drew his mouth to hers for a long, gentle kiss, putting all her hidden emotions in the wordless pledge of love.

"Then let's go to bed."

The telephone's shrill jangle shocked her awake. Beside her Nick's body stiffened as she lunged for the telephone, trying to prevent a second clamoring ring.

On the other end the news operator told Jordan she was needed on a story, and a hot surge of adrenaline shot through her. "Yes," Jordan replied without hesitation. It wasn't a huge story, she told herself as she put down the receiver, but it was the first. A start.

"Who was it?" Nick's voice was sleepy, but from the tightly controlled clip of his voice, she knew he already knew.

"I have to go." She threw back the covers and reached for the table lamp.

She glanced toward him and saw only his rigid jaw and narrowed obsidian eyes. The rest of his features were a hardened mask of fury.

"Call them back. Tell them to get Clayton."

The order pricked at her like needles of ice.

"I can't, Nick." When he bristled, her resolve wavered but she knew if she gave in this time, the first time, she'd give in every other time. She couldn't buy his love with complaisant obedience. She'd tried that before, and the cost had been too high. "It's part of my job, part of my life now."

"Dammit!" He leaped from the bed and stalked her with naked majesty. "Only the most experienced pilots ever take night calls. You know it's not worth going after, whatever it is."

"It's a plane crash on Superstition," she explained, heading toward the closet. "Explosion on impact. We'll get good footage." She looked at him steadily. "KPNX is going. So is KOOL."

"I don't care if every station in Arizona is going. I don't want you out there." He glanced at the luminous digits on her clock. "It's two o'clock in the damn morning. Look at you! You're so tired you can't even walk straight. You've no business flying at ni—"

"I can't walk straight because I'm trying to pull on my clothes and move at the same time." She took a slight hop as she stepped into the second leg of her panties. "You try it sometime and see—"

He grabbed the flight suit she'd pulled out of her closet and threw it on the bed. "I've done it a hundred, maybe a thousand times. How do you think I know what it's like up there? Do you think I assimilated it by osmosis? I've been there! Night maneuvers, S and R, flying by the seat of my pants and sheer willpower just high enough above the trees to keep from shaving off a few limbs, so damned tired I—"

He raked his fingers through his hair. She could feel his eyes boring into her as she backed to the bed, reaching for the rumpled flight suit.

When she stepped into the white uniform, his shoulders sagged. He sighed a long hiss of air.

"Stay with me tonight, Jordan. I'm leaving in the morning."

She longed to give in, to wrap herself in his warmth and hold him close until . . . Until he left. The words reverberated through her head. Until he left.

Lord! Here she was, agonizing over leaving him for a few hours when he had no qualms about his own departure. And he'd be gone for days.

She played his game.

"Don't leave in the morning."

"What?"

"Don't leave." She threw up her hands as if to wave away the problem. "Stay. Let someone else go to L.A., or let one of the executives there handle things."

He looked at her sharply and began to rummage through the pile of clothing they'd brought from the living room. He pulled on his briefs and slacks as she finished dressing.

"You know I can't do that," he said tightly. He jammed a sockless foot into a gray docksider.

"Why not?" she persisted. "Because the company will fall apart without you?"

"That's not it and you know it."

"You're right. That's not it. You *want* to go. You have to be in on every decision, every rudimentary process." She walked to the bathroom, with Nick hot on her heels, and she yanked a brush through her hair. "It's perfectly okay, in your book, for you to leave for days. It's business. It's your career. It's your livelihood." She watched him in the mirror, trying to gauge the impact of her words. "Well, this is my career. My livelihood. And I have to go." She edged past him into the hall and went to the living room in search of her purse.

His voice followed her. "It's not the same. I'm not risking my life!"

"Neither am I!"

"Jordan!"

She turned to find him standing at the front door, fully dressed.

"I'll follow you to the station," he said. "But I won't wait for you and I won't come back here. If I'd wanted to sleep alone, I could have done it in my own bed."

She listened to the clatter of his feet on the stairs as he bounded down the steps. Then she drew a deep, ragged breath, and tried not to believe this was the end.

Nine

Only a few more minutes, Jordan told herself, and she could put the worst part of the nightmare behind her. She pushed down on the collective pitch stick and felt the throttle of the jet-powered helicopter retard. The vibration of the rotor blades rippled through her, releasing the close-held pain in her heart to permeate her entire being. It was almost impossible to differentiate between her anguish at the sight of the fireball burning itself into the side of the mountain and her tormenting fear of losing Nick. Both were shattering finalities that, despite her frantic self-assurances to the contrary, she wasn't prepared to accept.

With concentrated effort she set the craft on the helipad and went through the motions of shutting down. She tried to focus on detail, on the hum of the rotors as they whirled to a stop, on the sure movements of her cameraman as he bounded from the chopper. But her mind kept straying to the tragedy on the mountain. And to the twin moons of Nick's headlights glancing off her rearview mirror as he'd followed her to the station. Followed her and then driven on.

A stream of light sliced through the Jet-Ranger windshield, and Jordan looked up as rectangular taillights fled from the parking lot. Her breathing stopped. It couldn't be Nick, she told herself. Even if the car had looked silver . . . She couldn't possibly figure out the color of the car. Not in the dark. Still, her heart wouldn't believe her. "It could have been Nick," it pounded, making hope stir and war with reason.

But it wasn't, she told herself again and again, while she scripted the story, while she drove home to her lonely bed. He wouldn't have driven off like that as soon as she touched down. Not if he'd been waiting. Not if . . . unless . . .

Stop it! she told herself. Even if he had been there, he'd left. At last, exhaustion put an end to her mental torture, and she fell into the deep, impenetrable black of sleep.

Her eyes flew open at the exact moment Nick's plane was due to take off; as if the Fates had poked her with unkind fingers and told her it was time for her to suffer some more. She listened to the silence, wondering how she could breathe with such a crushing weight on her chest. The pain was much worse this morning, she realized. The scent of him clung to her sheets, her pillows, making each moment of what should have been slumbering bliss wide-eyed anguish. It was his fault, she reasoned, trying to displace pain with anger. His fault she couldn't sleep, his fault she was hurting, his fault she was beginning to doubt her judgment in taking the call-out.

She forced her body out of bed and walked to the bathroom to stare at the swollen pockets under her bleary eyes. Fortunately she didn't have to go back to the station today. She wouldn't be able to fake it. But she needed to keep busy, to do something to keep from surrendering to self-pity.

She attacked the apartment with a vengeance, stopping only to watch her spot on the noon broadcast. It was good, she knew, but watching it left her feeling flat and defeated, as if, no matter how good she was, it still wasn't enough.

When the apartment was dangerously close to being spotless, she decided to go to the laundromat. Anything to keep from facing the quiet, from thinking too much. She gathered up several days' worth of soiled clothing, but couldn't bring herself to strip the bed. Nick was there. His scent. His memory.

On her second trip to the car she got the eerie feeling that someone was watching her. She'd just placed the basket in the passenger seat and stepped back to close the door when the tingling started.

"Jordan?"

Her heart slammed against her ribs and she did a slow half-turn, telling herself she was hallucinating. Nick was gone. Nick was in L.A. Nick was . . .

"What are you doing here?"

He was wearing an open-neck shirt and jeans. Those wonderfully tight, low-slung jeans that took her breath away.

"I take it you're still speaking to me?" he said softly.

The intimacy of his tone pulled at feelings that stung.

"I'm not sure."

"Then I guess I'll have to do most of the talking." A hesitant smile edged to the corners of his mouth. "You can just listen."

The battle between her heart and her brain was a short one, but surrender didn't come easily. Pride surged and fortified her crumbling heart. "I . . . I was on my way to do some laundry," she announced, as if it were a feat of great importance.

"I noticed that. While I was sitting in my car."

"Why weren't you sitting on an airplane? Why aren't you in L.A?"

A flicker of something almost like pain darted across his face. "I did a lot of thinking last night, and decided to take your advice about letting someone there handle things." He shrugged as if he delegated authority every day. "We need to talk."

He brushed his forehead with the back of his hand, and Jordan noticed for the first time that he was sweating. The thought came to her that he was nervous, but she pushed it aside. It was hot, that was all.

"Why don't you bring your laundry to my place?" he said, lifting his brows in inquiry. "We can talk there." His smile returned. "I'll even help you sort and fold."

It was almost too easy; the swift return to old playfulness, the flirtatious smile. Though her heart wanted to go, to see Nick's home, to accept his offer of truce, her sense of self-preservation warned her not to expect too much.

"All right," she agreed slowly. "But I'll follow you," she hastened to add when he started to remove the laundry baskets from her car. A small thing, she knew, but after the emotional whirlwind she'd been on for the last sixteen hours, she needed the security of having something in her control, even if it was only her car.

As she followed him down the palm-shaded streets of her neighborhood, the rectangular flash of his brake lights winked familiar greetings. It *was* him last night! Every chamber of her heart knew it with unshadowed certainty. A wave of elation washed through her, as if the proof of his commitment had just announced itself in brilliant red lettering. For the first time in what seemed like years, she took a deep, even breath and relaxed.

Though she knew Nick lived in the exclusive Scottsdale area, she was unprepared for his home: A winding drive through a small forest of pine, spruce, and fir led to a neat, two-story glass-and-stone house and circled in front of a covered walk leading to double front doors. The house was surrounded by native growth and various-sized outcroppings, but there was a balance, an eye-pleasing sense of precision to what should have been unruly. It was the bursts of displaced color that told Jordan of the hours of careful landscaping needed to give the aura of artless perfection. Splashes of vermilion and violet and yellow announced that human hands had worked alongside nature to sculpt the picturesque setting.

"It's beautiful, Nick," Jordan sighed, answering the silent question in his eyes as he opened her car door.

He held out his hand, and hers reached for his familiar strength. The intimate twining of their fingers consoled her, reaffirmed the bonds forged in more passionate joinings. For a few heavenly moments she forgot the anguish of the night before. But as Nick led her toward the house, she remembered why they were there and her self-confidence ebbed.

"I want to show you my pride and joy," Nick said, leading her to the front door. He punched a series of numbers into a small security device.

"We'll take a tour of the inside after you see this." He didn't give her time to admire the native rock foyer or the high-ceilinged, open rooms. He drew her through the house to a bright, sunlit area that overlooked the backyard. Beyond a triple set of sliding glass doors was a breathtaking panorama of nature and sky and water.

Water? Jordan did a double-take to assure herself she wasn't hallucinating. True, she reminded herself as she took in the sparkling ripples of diamond-laced blue, pools weren't exactly unusual. In fact, they were more or less expected in Scottsdale. But this? This was something out of Eden or paradise lost. Knee-high waterfalls cascaded into an enormous pool lined with native stone. A very deep pool, if the height of the diving platform towering next to a three-foot springboard was an accurate gauge.

Jordan followed Nick outside onto a large, wooden deck and absorbed the lush surroundings. When Nick had told her he swam a little, he'd failed to mention he did it in such splendor. Evergreens shaded and guarded the quiet coolness. The sharp tang of their spicy fragrance tickled her senses. No wonder Nick referred to this as his pride and joy. He'd created his own private oasis.

"Like it?"

He laughed at the look she gave him, and she knew he'd read the envious delight in her eyes.

"Now I know why you're in such good shape," she admitted, stunned by the surge of embarrassment she felt at mentioning something so intimate. Lord! She hated this sense of awkward unease, this sudden shifting of emotions. She felt as if she were on a first date instead of talking with the man she'd been making love with—was it only yesterday?

"The only question," she continued, wanting to shift the conversation to a less inflammable subject, "is how do you ever manage to drag yourself away?"

"I don't really know." His voice was low and earnest, his expression pensive. "I guess after a while it's natural to start taking things for granted." He looked directly into her eyes. "That's always a mistake. Sometimes we need to be reminded of that."

Jordan knew he meant he'd been taking much more than the house for granted, and waited for him to continue.

"Ready to see the rest?" he asked in a sudden shift of mood, knocking her off balance again. She didn't feel capable of keeping up with him today. She was still too emotionally bruised from their argument.

She accompanied him through the house, always aware of his strong body idling close by while she absorbed the beauty of his home. Although the house was much larger than it appeared from outside, it was just as inviting. Even the master bedroom, which she'd expected to be dark and masculine, was warmed by splashes of melon within variegated shades of blue. For a few quiet moments she pretended it was their bedroom, their bed, a secluded refuge they shared. But it was only pretense.

As the informal tour ended, she could no longer ignore a persistent little gremlin that was ruining her appreciation of Nick's home. It was the kitchen that shook her most and made her start wondering who had added all the soft, feminine touches. Nick might be able to cook well enough to fend for himself, but she couldn't picture him standing in the housewares department picking out dish towels and washcloths to coordinate with the wallpaper.

She picked up one of the towels and approached Nick with forced lightness. "Oh, Nick! This is so you!"

He laughed, as she'd intended, when he saw the cute little duck that graced the cloth. "That must be one of Rita's selections."

"Rita?"

"The woman who cooks and keeps house for me. I kind of leave it to her to keep things up around here. I, ah, haven't been home too much lately." His eyes got that heavy, heated look, and she knew he was thinking of where he'd been spending his free time.

She teetered on falling into the web of his sensuality. It would be easy to give in to the silken pull, to wrap herself in his arms and cling to the scent and feel of him. But suspicious jealousy waved its cooling hand over the welcome of the house and settled in her thoughts, thoughts that weren't much more than nebulous feelings before she spoke.

"Did your wife choose the colors for the house?"

"Veronica?" His black brows arched in surprise, and he leveled an intense look at her. "No. We'd been divorced long before I started building out here." He paused as he led her into the den and pulled her down beside him on the huge beige couch. "As a matter of fact, Carolyn Brierly did most of the decorating."

Jordan thought she might be ill. "Carolyn Brierly? I had no idea she was so talented," she finally managed.

Nick looked at her with surprise. "Surely you've heard of Brier Rose Designs?"

Jordan's ego took a direct hit. "Of course I've heard of it. I just didn't realize Carolyn had any connection."

He pinned Jordan with an unwavering look. "She did a good job on the house, wouldn't you say?"

She closed her eyes to shut out the image of cool, tawny-maned Carolyn, and focused on the house. Warm colors washed over her, masculine and feminine, soft and hard, blending, yielding one unto the other.

"Yes, she did an excellent job."

"This was one of her first commissions," Nick continued, expanding on a subject Jordan would just as soon drop. "She was so frantic over every detail that for a while I thought I'd made a mistake in giving her the job." He gave a low chuckle and stretched his arms along the back of the sofa, eyeing his domain like a pleased sultan. His right hand curved over Jordan's shoulder, and he coaxed her to lean into his solid chest. "Only Steven saved my sanity. And Carolyn's commission."

"How'd he manage that?" Jordan asked, relaxing in slow degrees. Nick's body heat was like a narcotic. Nothing would feel more wonderful than to curl up against him and rest. Well, almost nothing, she amended, when Nick's hand grazed the side of her breast as he draped his arm around her. She snuggled a little closer, feeling the warmth of his body seep into her soul.

"He developed a rather strong interest in interior design and offered to run interference for me. I was delighted to let him help me out."

"Does Steven still like design?" She noticed with detached interest that her words didn't sound quite right and that her eyelids were getting very heavy.

Her head moved with his chest as Nick chuckled. "No. Steven's passion for that disappeared about the same time he stopped dating Carolyn's assistant. But by then the worst was over, and Carolyn was relaxed enough to accept the truth when I told her I was really happy with her work."

His hands moved over her hair in slow, soothing strokes. Jordan knew she shouldn't give in to the exhaustion pressing in on her. They needed to talk. She tried to lift her head, but gentle hands urged her to stay nestled.

"I want you to stay close to me for a few more minutes," Nick said softly. "I want to get back a few of the minutes we lost last night."

Last night began to have less and less significance as she surrounded herself with the scent and feel of him. Nothing else held any importance when they were together like this, just the two of them, holding each other.

"I missed you." She sighed. "I missed this."

"So did I. More than I imagined possible." He

shifted—restlessly, she thought. "It made me do a lot of thinking."

She could feel his body tense. Was missing her so terrible that it upset him? Had last night caused him to question her importance in his life? Her own nerves began to strain. "Nick, if this is about the call-out." She lifted a hand to his chest, reveling in the heat and strength she found there. "I know how you feel about my flying—"

His mirthless laugh interrupted her. "No, you don't. Not really." His chest heaved with a sigh. "It hasn't been so bad lately—during the day. But I knew, even before it happened, that nights would be different. Nights would be hell. And I was right. Every second you were up there, all I could see was . . ." A slight tremor rippled through him. "But worried or not, I shouldn't have started an argument just before you had to take off. That was arrogant stupidity on my part. If anything had happened—"

She touched her fingers to his mouth. "Nothing did, and nothing will. I'm careful, Nick. I don't take chances."

He nodded, and after placing a brief kiss on her fingers, tucked them back against his chest.

"I'll get better," he promised. "At least I'll try." He gave a rueful laugh. "I guess I'll have to, if I don't want to lose you. But that's only part of what I wanted to talk to you about."

He took a deep breath. "When we first met, I told you about my marriage. What I didn't tell you was that its failure was mostly my fault." His voice was tight, matching the rigid set of his body. "I didn't give Veronica the time, the consideration, a woman deserves. I always put business first, flying off to one city or another, leaving her alone. If I'd spent more time with her, been with her on those nights when she needed someone . . . well, who knows? But there were too many nights apart, too many days when she didn't know whether I'd come home or not, too many disagreements left unsettled."

His arm left her, and Jordan knew from the way his chest rose that he was raking his fingers through his hair. She wished she could do, or say, something to ease his tension, but she didn't want to risk interrupting his rare openness. It was a gift too precious to risk losing.

"What I'm getting at is that this"—his arm encircled her again and tightened with emphasis— "this relationship is very important to me. I don't want the same thing to happen to us."

"Oh, Nick!" She lifted her chin and buried her face in the curve of his neck, breathing in his scent as relief and joy washed through her. "Neither do I."

He eased away from her and placed a hand on either side of her face, tilting her head so she was looking directly into his sable eyes. "We need to be together. We belong together. Nothing should interfere with that."

Jordan watched his face as he spoke, mesmerized by his sincerity. It was there in his eyes, in his voice, in his touch. It lifted her heart and sent it soaring. She nodded her agreement, certain that everything he was going to say was everything she wanted to hear. Words like "I love you," and "marry me," filled the room with silent tension, and she waited . . . waited for him to say what was in his heart.

She felt the tension flow from his body, and he released his hold on her. His smile was wide and brilliant, as if he'd just discovered the sun. He stood quickly, and she followed his movements with her eyes, unwilling to lose a single second of these glorious moments with so much as a blink.

"I think we should live here, don't you?" His smile became sheepish. "That laundry was a great excuse for getting you out here to see the house. I can't tell you the relief I felt when you said you loved it."

Jordan stared at him, expectantly. Soon, she told herself, he'd say the words. He was just happy, too excited to realize he'd left the most important things unsaid. She smiled at him in gentle understanding.

"It'll be so perfect. We can spend every spare moment together. If I have to go out of town for any length of time, you can meet me on your days off, or just pack up and go with me."

Shadows of confusion dimmed the brightness of her happiness. Go with him? But she waved the tentative problems aside. They'd work all that out. Being with him, growing closer day by day, year by year, was all she wanted to think about now. Not her career.

"When do you think you can move in?"

"Move in?"

Nick looked at her with wry affection. "How can we start living together if you don't move in?"

She felt as if she were turning to stone. Her mouth froze in a disbelieving smile. "Live together?" The words she knew had come from her sounded as if they'd been spoken from somewhere far away.

"I . . . I . . ." Words wouldn't come. Everything ceased to function as his meaning crashed down on her, demolishing her happiness. He wasn't proposing marriage. He wasn't speaking of love and commitment, just convenience. His convenience.

Pain and pride clawed at her heart, lurched through her stomach. She sat perfectly still, afraid to move, afraid to let go of the rigid control she needed to keep from shattering. She felt the sofa give under Nick's weight as he sat beside her and took her hands in his. "You look a little frazzled, sweetheart. Have I taken you that much by surprise?"

She knew she was looking right at him, but for some reason she couldn't see him clearly. His body was a dark shadow, his face featureless. She blinked, trying to get her eyes, her mind, to focus. To her horror, a fat tear splashed down her cheek. She averted her face, hoping Nick hadn't seen. She didn't want him to know how hurt she was, how foolish she'd been.

"Jordan?" His voice was soft, hesitant.

She forced a tight smile and looked in his direction, but not at him. She couldn't bear that. Not until the pain subsided.

"I'm just so tired." A sob lodged in her throat, and she disguised it as a strained laugh. "And I've been so . . . uptight. Yes," she said truthfully, finally managing to look at him. "This whole idea is quite a surprise."

"I'm sorry. I've been thinking about it so much, it seems like old news to me. I guess I was a little clumsy with it."

"No. No. It's just that . . ." She closed her eyes and tried to put her thoughts in order. But nothing came except the mounting urgency to leave;

to get up and walk away from this, put some distance between herself and Nick. "It's just that I need to think this out."

She could tell he didn't understand her lack of enthusiasm, could see the flash of pained surprise that crossed his face.

"Yeah, well, I guess I couldn't expect you to jump into it without giving it some thought. I know you don't like to be pushed, but I thought . . . when you said . . ."

He shoved a hand through his hair and pushed himself up to stand, looking around the room as if trying to find the answer to her hesitation hidden there.

"We can redecorate, if you want. Whatever you think. It doesn't matter." His voice took on a forced animation. "You can change the furniture. The carpet. Hell," he said with a tight laugh, "change it all. I want you to be happy here."

"It's lovely just as it is. That's not it."

"Then what is it, dammit? What?"

Ten

The sharp edge in his voice was the final wound. She couldn't do this anymore, couldn't hold back the tears, the pain, the disappointment. Jordan surged to her feet, and dashed away the teardrops that spilled from her eyes.

"It's not enough, that's what it is," she said shakily. "It's just not enough. I need more than a temporary roof over my head, a warm body to hold me at night. That may be enough for you, but it's not for me. I need to have love, Nick. I need to feel—"

She couldn't go on when she looked at his face, pale and strained. A stranger's face regarding her with a stranger's eyes. He stared at her as if he'd never seen her before.

"I guess I read this all wrong," he said, the cold ring of his voice splintering through her like shards of ice. "I thought we had something pretty special going for us. I thought you felt that way too."

"I do," Jordan sobbed, dangerously close to losing her fragile control.

"But not enough. Right?"

She inhaled at the glancing blow. "That's not what I meant. Please, try to understa—"

"Oh, I understand all right," he said with a cynical laugh. His hands balled into tight fists at his sides. "I was stupid enough to think what we had was pretty damned good. The best. But apparently I'm the only one who sees it that way." The angry fire in his eyes flamed higher. "I thought, God, I thought—"

He broke off and stared at her, his body drawn up in a tight stance. The muscle in his jaw ticked madly. He looked like a statue brought to life by the Furies, gathering all the light and energy that surrounded him. She could see him struggling for control, as if he sensed the wild power erupting through him. Then he sighed, a long, shuddering breath, and the light drained, leaving only the cold, lifeless statue.

He closed his eyes, and his voice sounded hollow and empty when he spoke. "I'm sorry, Jordan. Honesty shouldn't be rewarded with anger." He opened his eyes and pushed a hand through his hair. "I was just so sure . . . I thought that if we gave it enough time, the feelings you want would just . . ." His shoulders rose and his hands spread in a searching gesture. ". . . just come."

"Just come?" She wanted to shake him and hold him all at the same time. "Oh, Nick. If they haven't come by now, what makes you think they ever will?"

He flinched and looked away, but Jordan knew he'd never find the answers he was seeking. They just weren't there. The bleak despair in his eyes when he looked back at her told her as surely as the aching pain in her soul that he knew it too. The love, the commitment she needed, just weren't there.

She tried to comfort him with a smile, but her lips only quivered, and she knew she couldn't bear it another moment. She couldn't be brave and understanding. Knowing that he didn't want to hurt her, didn't choose not to love her, didn't diminish her pain. She whirled, stepping out blindly in her urgency to escape.

She was almost grateful when her leg struck the sharp edge of the coffee table and she could release a strangled whimper.

Nick was at her side before she could think, the gentleness of his touch more painful than her wounded knee. He helped her ease down on the sofa, and the burning sting when she bent her knee sharpened her senses. She looked up, captured by the soft concern in his eyes.

"Let me get a wet cloth," he murmured. "I'll be right back." With a sad imitation of a smile, he brushed her face lightly, catching a tear as it slipped down her cheek. He touched his finger to his lips, tasting her sorrow.

"Don't cry," he whispered. "We'll work it out."

Her hungry eyes watched as he disappeared down the hall, and she knew she was losing a part of herself. How could she bear it without him? But she knew she would. And the irony of it was that he was the one who had given her that knowledge. He had proven to her that she was whole and complete just as she was; never asking for more than she was willing to give and always content with what she offered. Until today. And even now, he wasn't asking too much. He just wasn't asking enough.

She waited until she heard him rummaging through the guest bath before she struggled to her feet and quietly let herself out of the house.

"What the hell happened to you?"

Clayton's gaze followed her across the room as Jordan limped to her desk. She settled into her chair and absently picked up the first thing she could find, darting a glance at Clayton's expectant face. "I had a little accident yesterday."

"A car wreck?"

"No. I cut my knee on a glass table," she explained, wondering if he could tell that her knee was the least of it.

"Must be giving you fits. You look like hell."

She closed her eyes to hide a sudden sting of tears and forced a dry laugh. She should look like hell. That's where she was. "Thanks a lot, Clay. You're a real gentleman."

· "I'm serious, Jordan. You look bad. Maybe you should go home."

"No! I mean . . ." She paused to still her racing heart. She didn't want to go home. How could she bear to go into her bedroom again and face her lonely bed, or go into the dining room and look at the brightly polished table, Nick's first gift to her, knowing the memories would still be there but he wouldn't? She couldn't go back and face all that again. "I'll be fine, Clayton. Really."

She didn't miss the assessing look he shot her.

"Well, you sure aren't going to do any flying today."

Her shoulders sagged, and she ran a shaking hand over her face. "I know." She'd fooled herself all morning into thinking it might be possible, but after driving to work, she'd known her leg was too stiff to work the foot pedals. She'd be grounded until her knee was mobile enough to ensure perfect coordination. But, Lord, how she wanted to fly; to soar up into the sky and try to outrun the pain. She stared sightlessly at the papers in her hand before placing them back on the desk. "I guess I'll go give Steven the good news."

"Stay put. I'll tell him." He glared a warning when she started to protest. "You need to stay off that leg."

Jordan slumped back in her chair with a heavy sigh. She needed to stay off her leg. She needed to be at home. She needed to be able to breathe without hurting, and to keep her eyes from filling with tears every other second. She needed lots of things, but most of all, she needed Nick.

Give it time, she told herself. Time heals all wounds. But she knew it was a lie. Some pains ran too deep. Some wounds never healed; especially self-inflicted ones.

Why had she done it? she asked herself for what seemed the millionth time. Why hadn't she just taken what he'd offered and been happy with that for as long as it lasted? Why not postpone the pain for a few weeks, or months, or years?

She tried again to envision living with Nick with no commitment. Would they go their separate ways when his passion cooled? Or would they stay together, drifting into marriage, Nick settling for what was comfortable and familiar?

No. She couldn't do that. She wanted love; she had to be sure that despite her faults she was needed, not settled for.

"Hey, lady. What's this I hear about your being wounded?"

Steven's voice jerked her out of her pondering and drew her gaze to his lanky frame. Her heart lurched as she took in the thick mane of wavy black hair, the broad, muscular chest. So like Nick. Too much like Nick. She averted her gaze.

"Just a little battle scar," she quipped, her voice low and shaky.

"Not too little, from the look on your face. Roll up your pant leg and let me see it." He knelt by her chair and gently lifted her leg. "Doesn't look too bad," he said, examining her knee. "But it's pretty swollen. You'd better keep it elevated all you can." He pulled out a desk drawer and lifted her extended limb onto the convenient prop.

"Now I know why Nick called this morning and told me to keep an eye on you." His chocolate-brown eyes glittered. "You're dangerous on your own."

Jordan thought her chest would explode before she could breathe again. "Nick called?"

"Yeah. All the way from L.A. just to tell me to look after you." He smiled and winked. "It's no secret . . ."

Jordan scarcely heard anything beyond the fact that Nick was in Los Angeles. Gone! He was gone. She wouldn't be able to catch so much as a glimpse of him. She'd thought, stupidly, that she'd really let go, but now Jordan knew she'd been carrying hope around like an invisible shield. Hoping when she saw him today something would be different, that he'd take one look at her and realize how much he loved her, needed her, how perfect she was for him. But now those secret hopes had to be relinquished. He was gone!

"Jordan?"

The urgency in Steven's voice trapped her attention. His face, taut with concern, came into focus.

"You're pale as a ghost. I'm taking you home right now."

"I don't need to go home. I'm fine."

"Right." He took her hands in his and studied her intently. "You faded out on me, Jordan. You have to be in a lot of pain."

"I'll recover," she tried to assure him. "And I didn't fade out. I heard every word you said."

He inclined his head, his eyes challenging her statement. "So who's the new station manager?"

She stared at him blankly.

"I just spent a good three minutes extolling the virtues of Dan Brown, giving you a cheery little pep talk about how Nick and I can turn the operation over to him and—" He sighed with exasperation. "Home, Jordan."

And suddenly that seemed the place to be. If Nick wasn't going to be here, she didn't want to be either.

Steven made arrangements for her car, then escorted her to his. She sat meekly staring out the window while he drove her home.

When they reached her apartment, Steven helped her up the stairs, and once they were inside, he insisted she stretch out on the couch.

"Is there anything you need?"

"No," she said listlessly. "Nothing."

He snapped his fingers and glanced around the living room. "I know what'll cheer you up! Where's your phone?"

"What for?"

"To call Nick. He'll—"

"No!"

His eyes rounded in surprise, confusion plainly written on his handsome features. Then, slowly, his expression changed to one of awareness.

"It's not your knee, is it?" He waited patiently for her response.

"No," she said, clearing her throat to hide the thickness in her voice.

He moved across the room to sit beside her on the sofa, looking at her with gentle understanding.

"Want to talk about it?"

"There's nothing to say." Her bottom lip started to tremble. "It's over."

"Over?" A frown creased his brow as he considered her words, then he slowly shook his head. "A man like Nick doesn't ask his brother to look after a woman he no longer cares about. And you wouldn't go all pale and weepy-eyed at the mention of his name if it were over."

She sighed, sniffed, sighed again. "You just don't know."

"So tell me."

"He . . . he wanted me to move in with him," she whispered, looking down at her hands.

"That's it? He wanted you to move in with him, and now it's over?" He paused. "Ah, now I see. You don't love him."

Her head snapped up. "Of course I love him."

"Then what's the problem?"

Jordan suddenly felt bone-tired. The sleepless night, the hours of crying, caught up with her. Her eyelids slid shut as she tried to vocalize the painful truth. "He doesn't love me," she said finally. "He only"—her throat tightened on the words—"wants me."

"Of course he wants you. Anyone who's ever seen him look at you knows that. But if you think he doesn't love you, for my money, you're dead wrong."

Her heart tilted crazily, and she was helpless against the swirl of hope that filled her chest. She was afraid to open her eyes, afraid she might see doubt instead of the certainty she heard.

She felt the cushion under her hips resettle as Steven rose to his feet.

"If there's one thing I know, Jordan, it's my brother. He's the only family I've had for most of my life. I spent years trying to be like him; watching, studying, learning. There's very little about Nick I don't understand. Forgive me, but I know he's had a lot of women in his life."

Her eyes flew open with the sharp sting of his honesty.

"And not once," he continued, capturing her gaze, "not once since he gave up on his marriage, has he ever asked a woman to share anything more than his bed. If he's asked you to live with him, he's asking you to share his life. That's as close to admitting love as he may ever get."

She closed her heart to his words. "If he loved me, he'd say so. He's never been shy about letting me know what he feels."

"Feels? Or wants? There's a world of difference in those two words. Anyone who's spent five minutes with Nick knows what he wants. He's never been able to hide his drive. But not many people know why. And that has to do with feelings. Nick's always been an expert at hiding those."

"Why?" she pleaded, wishing she could understand and accept, as Steven seemed to.

Steven rolled his shoulders and dragged a hand along the back of his neck. "I think it's too hard for him. Nick can do just about anything—hell, in my eyes, everything. But he can't put his feelings into words. He keeps them close. But they're there. For anyone to see who'll take the time to look."

"I looked!"

"Did you really? Or did you just listen?" He pulled his keys from his pocket and gave her a small smile. "Some men are only as good as their words, Jordan. And for some men, actions speak loudest. I think Nick said it loud and clear. You just haven't learned to read sign language yet."

She thought about that long after Steven left, tried to recall all the times she'd wondered, hoped, almost believed, Nick loved her. There'd been so many. But always, she'd quelled them, because Nick hadn't said it, hadn't said the words she so longed to hear. But then, her heart reminded her with a surge of hope, neither had she. She'd wanted to, so many times; had felt it with every fiber of her being. But she'd never said the words.

Her spirits soared higher before another crushing realization sent them hurtling downward. Even if he did love her, it wasn't enough. Love meant commitment. Love meant forever. Nick had offered her only *now*. If he did love her, his love wasn't strong enough for him to offer forever. And that's what she wanted. Forever.

Jordan didn't know exactly when she started to cry. It might have been the moment she stepped inside the small wedding chapel, hushed and tranquil, yet filled with a spirit of joy and love. Or maybe the music had pulled the salty mist from her heart. Or Mark, proud and nervous as he waited at the altar. Or maybe she was just crying for herself again. For the life she'd never have with Nick.

She fought a fresh burst of tears as Delia took her place beside Mark and they began reciting their vows. Such beautiful words she thought, listening to the promises she had once repeated with fervent solemnity. She'd expected it to last forever, but it hadn't worked out that way.

So many weddings. So many failures. Maybe Mark and Delia would be two of the lucky ones. She hoped so. With a little luck and a lot of love, they just might make it, might hold on through the ups and downs, might . . .

Might. The word reverberated through her melancholy, cleansing and clarifying. They might make it, they might not. It took more than an exchange of vows to commit for a lifetime. Marriage was no guarantee, no promise of forever. It was only a promise to try.

Everything around her faded, the ceremony, the crowded pews. There was only her heart, lifting, swirling, pounding with renewed life. And her certainty. Her joyous, frightening certainty that she'd had her promise of forever, her promise to try, and she hadn't heard it. She just hadn't been listening.

Giddy excitement meshed with mounting terror as Jordan parked her car next to Nick's in the wide circular drive of his home. All the dark thoughts that had tried to insinuate themselves throughout the drive to Scottsdale converged in a hammering fear that ripped through her courage. What if he didn't want to see her? What if his feelings, the ones she was only assuming existed in the first place, had died as easily as hers had grown? He'd made no effort to contact her in the days since he'd returned from Los Angeles. What if she was making a fool of herself? What if . . .

Stop it, she ordered, rejecting the thoughts in another wash of optimism. It would be all right. She heaved a shaking sigh. Please, please, let it be all right.

She almost changed her mind when she reached his front door. The silence, the horrifying sense of absolute stillness, surrounded her, amplifying the pounding of her heart. Only the image of Nick, and the stranglehold of her hope, allowed her to subdue her clamoring insecurities and reach for the doorbell.

By the third ring, she knew it was pointless. He wasn't there; wasn't waiting, pacing, praying for her to come. Fool, she chided, moving woodenly toward her car. Idiot! Making up comforting scenarios of eager arms reaching for her, warm lips—

An almost imperceptible sound penetrated her thoughts. She stopped, holding her breath, straining to place the fragmented noise. It came again. A muffled . . . splash?

Summoning all her courage, Jordan walked to the back of the house, her breathing constricted by nervous excitement. She passed through the wrought-iron gate with scarcely a thought to the absence of a lock. Her senses were flooded, churning with fear and anticipation.

She rounded the corner of the house, and an

image of bronzed sinew, suspended for a breathtaking instant against the cloudless blue sky, filled her eyes. The vision arched and hurled downward, disappearing into the sparkling aquamarine depths yawning below.

Nick's head broke the surface of the water, and his powerful arms pulled him across the length of the pool. Just the sight of him sent pulses of love and desire washing through her. She clung to a stone jutting from the side of the house, watching him slice the water with smooth, even strokes.

When he reached the near end of the pool, she pushed herself away from the sheltering rock, her desire to be near him stronger than the anxiety that turned her legs to Jell-O.

"Nick," she called tentatively. She wasn't certain she'd spoken loudly enough for him to hear, but wasn't certain she wanted to.

He *had* heard. His body jerked as if he'd been shot, and his head whipped in her direction. Jordan prayed she wasn't misreading the brightness that lighted his eyes, the lightning-quick flash of pleasure.

She took another step toward him. "Hi," she said nervously. The word sounded more like a croak than a greeting.

Nick hauled himself out of the pool in a single fluid motion, his gaze never wavering. Beads of water ran like shimmering diamonds along the muscled planes of his body, and Jordan fought an overwhelming need to imitate their intimate caresses.

"Hi, yourself," he said in a quiet voice, finally allowing his gaze to move over her. She held still for his scrutiny, using the moments to drink in every detail of his face; absorbing the new leanness in his cheeks, the slight deepening of the tiny lines that fanned from his eyes and knotted around her heart.

"You look tired," she ventured, when his gaze once again sought hers.

His hand brushed away a drop of water that fell from his hair toward his temple. "Yeah," he agreed, his voice sounding deeper than she remembered. "I haven't been sleeping too well lately." A mirthless smile formed on his lips. "For about the past week or so.

"You look wonderful." His gaze roamed her mauve silk blouse and lace dirndl skirt. "What's the occasion?"

She cleared her throat to disguise the huskiness generated by his approving perusal. "The wedding," she managed. "Mark and Delia's."

"Oh, yeah," he said, nodding. "I, uh, I couldn't make it." A strained silence passed. "What are you doing here?" The quiet intensity of his voice shook her.

She tucked her trembling fingers in the folds of her skirt and slid them nervously over the jagged patterns of lace. "I . . . I wanted to see you." Her gaze flew over his muscled form and the red-and-white striped, and very brief, swimming trunks. She ran her tongue across suddenly dry lips. "I mean," she corrected, training her eyes on his face, "I wanted to talk to you."

"About what?" Every muscle in his neck and shoulders tautened as he stared down at her. "I think you said it all last week."

She took a deep breath. "I made a mistake," she said on a shaky exhalation. "I thought it wouldn't be enough. Just living together. But I was wrong. Oh, Nick, I was so wrong."

Her words hung in the air. He was so silent Jordan thought surely he must be listening to the frantic banging of her heart. She sucked in her bottom lip and bit down hard to keep the tears that welled in her eyes from spilling over.

"Nick?" Her hand moved toward him of its own volition, seeking the chiseled strength of his jaw.

He drew in a sharp hiss of breath. "It won't work," he bit out as a spasm of emotion crossed his face. "I can't go through this again." His hand closed over hers, and for a moment she thought he was pulling her closer. But almost as soon as she thought it, he stepped back and released her hand. His own splayed through his hair, and Jordan had to fight to keep her knees from buckling under the agony of his rejection.

"Don't you think I've wanted to go back too?" he asked, piercing her with his eyes. "Lord, Jordan, I've driven myself nearly crazy, thinking if I'd just given you more time, hadn't pushed so hard, hadn't backed you into a corner, you wouldn't have run out on me.

"I've gone over this again and again, trying to work things out, to make things different. But it always ends up the same." He looked away, but not before she caught the flash of pain in his eyes. "You just don't want the same things I do. Every time I try to get closer, you pull away. The more I want, the faster you run. Living together isn't going to change that."

"Nick—"

"No," he said with a slow shake of his head. "I can't take the risk again, Jordan. Your habit of running is too deep."

"Running? I'm not running, Nick." Her heart

banged in panicked flurry. "I'm here! I want to be with you, however you want me. We belong together."

"For how long, Jordan? Until I need you just a little too much? Until you decide again that what you feel just isn't enough?"

"Not enough?" She was in the middle of a nightmare, some incomprehensible nightmare. What was he talking about? Why was he looking at her with that stony resolve? Why wasn't he hearing her? "I love you, Nick!" The words burst from her in frantic desperation. "I love you."

For a moment his expression altered and she thought she saw triumph and joy chase one another across his face. But then, disbelief voiced itself in the tightening of his jaw, the wariness in his eyes. He seemed to pull into himself, to erect another wall, another barrier for her to cross.

"But not enough. Right, Jordan? Isn't that what last week was all about?" His voice was low, tight. "You love me enough to want to be with me, but any kind of commitment scares you to death. Well"—he gave her a smile to match his voice— "that's not love. As much as you'd like to think it—hell, as much as I'd like to believe it—that's not love. That's just plain old want."

"Don't you dare—" She clamped an iron vise around her emotions as frustration bled into outrage. She wanted to scream at him, vent her pain in a screeching rage. She took a step toward him, hands clenched for battle. "Don't you dare put your misguided qualifications on what I feel."

"Misguided?"

"I know the difference between love and lust," she continued, ignoring his questioning protest.

She took another step toward him, and to her irritation, he backed away. Her temper inched higher. She wanted to be nose-to-nose with him when she gave it to him with both barrels.

"I know what I feel and the way I feel it. Maybe you have a problem with semantics, but I don't." She inched forward until she had him trapped between herself and the pool. A soft whiff of his spiced scent cut through the chlorine sting in the air, softening her anger as she hugged the intimate fragrance to her senses. "I love you," she said, throwing pride and caution to the wind. "As in the forever kind, the commitment kind, the kind that goes deeper than glands and bedrooms. I know what I feel. What I don't know, what I have *never* known, is how you feel."

The look he shot her was laughably incredulous.

"You have to know!" he almost shouted. "I've done everything humanly possible to prove how much you mean to me. How many times have I *told* you how much I want you?"

"I'm not talking about what you *want*, Nick." Her tone was almost amused, as a lifting certainty pushed her misery aside. "I know you want me. I'm talking about what you *feel*."

He had the audacity to look disgruntled, as if he still didn't believe what she was saying, didn't know the words she desperately needed to hear. Well, she wasn't going to let him get away with it. If she let him withdraw now, it would set a pattern for the rest of their lives, and she had every confidence that the rest of their lives was exactly what they were dealing with. Everything he'd been saying, every misunderstood word, had finally soaked in. If it weren't for the enormity of the problem, she could almost laugh. But it was time for some straight talk. Right here, right now.

"Tell me, Nick," she demanded, holding him prisoner with her gaze. "Tell me what you feel."

His expression became cautious. "You have to know," he said softly, his eyes roaming the depths of hers.

"Did you know? Until I told you, did you have any idea how very much I love you?"

His expression gave little away, but it was enough.

"I'm just like you, Nick. I need to hear the words."

His eyes, so dark and mysterious, grew darker still with the emotions that stirred behind them. Jordan wanted to hold him, her need to feel him pressed against her was almost painful in its intensity. But that could come later, after they'd bridged the dangerous waters of learning to be open with each other, learning to speak what was in their hearts instead of letting the fires of passion speak for them.

She waited, her heart suspended in agonizing fear and expectation, for his heart to give her the words. And slowly, as soft as the kiss of summer winds, he gave them.

"I love you."

Tension flew out of her, while tears of relief and joy stung her eyes. "And I love you," she breathed, not knowing who reached for the other first, only knowing that she was finally back in his arms; back where she belonged.

Oblivious to her dampened clothes, she reveled in the feel of him, the scent of him, the absolute rightness of loving him. His hands traveled lovingly up and down her back, leaving a trail of flame in their wake. Her fingers tangled through the wet raven wings of his hair as she clung to her future, hearing his sweet words in the very darkest corner of her heart.

"I'll move in tomorrow," she promised, clinging to him, thinking the sudden tightening of his hold was his approval. "Or tonight." She nipped at his ear. "Or how 'bout right now?"

She arched her back and lifted her face, waiting for his mouth to claim hers. Her gaze sought his, wanting to record these precious moments, the electric seconds before she became lost in his taste.

The clouded caution in his eyes cast angry shadows over her happiness.

"No," he said quietly, setting her away from him with a firm grip on her upper arms. "It's still not enough."

She fought to steady runaway emotions. Surely he wasn't saying what she thought she heard. He wasn't saying he didn't want her, not now, not after—

"You said you loved me. The forever kind. The commitment kind."

She could only nod, dawning awareness lifting her lips in a tremulous smile.

"Sometimes words just aren't enough," he said, dropping his hands. "Prove how much you love me. And let me prove how much I love you. Every day, for the rest of our lives." His gaze probed hers with strained intensity. "Marry me."

Her heart nearly exploded with the impact of his words. She launched herself into his arms with a strangled cry of joy, knocking him off balance with the force of her happiness. She thought she was flying, soaring in the arms of her love into the clouds of her dreams—until the earthly chill of chlorinated water folded around her and tugged her down toward the bottom of the pool in a wild tangle of thrashing limbs.

They erupted to the surface at the same instant; coughing, choking, wiping at flooded eyes with soaking hands. Jordan sank again, the water-drenched weight of her clothes dragging her down. A muscular arm encircled her, lifting and pulling until she broke the surface. She finally stopped fighting the water when she realized she could touch bottom.

She used both hands to push her hair out of her eyes, which wasn't easy with Nick's arms closed around her. She felt an elbow clip his chin, a forearm scrape his shoulder. Her eyes popped open at his muffled gasp.

"Damn, Jordan," he sputtered, the laughing gleam in his eyes belying his tone. "Can I take that as a yes?"

Epilogue

Jordan ignored her comical grimace reflected in the bathroom mirror, and dabbed at the smear of mascara under her lower lashes.

"I hope that look isn't for me."

The sensuous baritone caressed her like a soothing breeze, and she turned toward its source. "Nick!" Her heart did its usual half-beat whenever she saw him after a day's separation, and she hurried into his waiting arms. "I didn't hear you come in."

"You know me. The strong, silent type." His last word was muffled as his mouth closed over hers. "Happy anniversary," he whispered, reluctantly breaking the kiss.

"Happy anniversary," she whispered back, knowing her erratic breathing matched his.

His hands smoothed down her back, pressing the cool silk of her slip against her skin, and he gave a low growl when his touch found the swell of her hips.

"If this is what you're wearing tonight, I heartily approve." He pulled back and swept her with a warm gaze. "As long as we stay home."

"You can't get out of it that easily," she teased. "You know we're expected at the benefit, anniversary or not."

He gave an exasperated sigh. "I know. But it's bad enough for you at any time, and tonight's—"

"I'll be fine. As long as you don't stray too far from my side."

"Never," he promised, placing a soft kiss on her forehead before turning to loosen his tie and shrug out of his suit jacket. "How was your day?"

"Oh-h-h-h . . . just fine." She followed him into their bedroom. "I took off early and ran a few errands."

"I know. Dan Brown called the office this afternoon." Nick's voice sounded almost too casual.

"He did?" She didn't have to fake surprise at the station manager's call. Blast Dan! She'd kill him!

"Yeah." Keeping his face averted, Nick walked to the closet and draped his jacket over a large wooden hanger. "He said you turned in your notice today."

"That rat! He wasn't supposed to tell you!"

"Jordan, I expect to be advised of all key personnel moves. Especially if that key person is my wife."

"But I wanted to tell you. To surprise you!"

"Oh, believe me," he said, crossing to the foot of their bed, "I was surprised." He watched her silently while he removed the rest of his clothing. "Why didn't you tell me you were thinking about quitting?"

"It was going to be one of my anniversary gifts. And I'm not quitting. Exactly." She searched for the best words, troubled by the frown that etched his brow. "As soon as I can, I'd like to learn the production end. I want to direct."

"You'd be good at that," he said softly, losing the worried look. "And your not flying anymore would be a wonderful gift to me. But are you sure this is what you want to do?"

She would have fallen in love with him all over again if if weren't impossible to love him more. She knew how much he wanted her to give up flight reporting, how much he hated the nights they spent at her old apartment when she was on call. Yet now that she was quitting, he worried that she might regret her decision.

"I'm sure."

His dark eyes flooded with light, but still he persisted. "You're sure you've thought it through carefully? That offer from KOOL won't be the only one, now that you've made such a name for yourself."

"I don't care," she said truthfully, walking toward him. His arms opened automatically, and she nestled her head against his chest. The wiry mat of hair tickled her chin, and she snuggled closer, breathing in the intoxicating scent of man and spice, warmed by the special blending so uniquely his. "I don't care if every station from Phoenix to Denver, with Atlanta thrown in, wants me. I don't need to prove myself anymore, Nick." She ran her hands over the familiar musculature of his back. "I haven't needed to since the day you said you loved me."

His fingers curved under her chin, and he tilted her head up. The eyes that sought hers were overly bright, liquid with emotion. Then his lashes lowered, hiding the depth of his feelings, but his descending mouth showed her with a language of its own. His lips parted hers, and his breath fanned warm against them before his tongue swept forward, gently tracing the inner curve of her mouth.

She sighed with him, opening herself to the growing exploration of his mouth. He claimed her offering, tasting her with mounting urgency. She pressed against him, measuring the muscled swell of his arms with outspread fingers on the journey to his neck, locking her arms about him as he lifted her hips, pressing her against his swelling desire.

A subtle pressure from his hands arched her back, and with his knee braced on the mattress, he lowered her to the bed.

"Nick!" she protested halfheartedly. "Dinner's almost ready and I have to get dress—"

His mouth silenced her, and his hand made a tantalizing foray from her waist to her breasts. "I want you for dinner," he said, teasing her nipple to a tight peak beneath the silken cover of her slip. "Besides"—his eyes took on an indefinable glow—"we agreed that you'd be a flight reporter until we were ready to start a family. Looks like I'll have to get busy on my half of the deal, since you jumped the gun just a little."

The magic of his hands and mouth pulled a pleasured moan from deep within her, and she helped him work her slip, the only barrier between her hungry skin and his ravenous mouth, down her shoulders and past her hips. Her plan to tell him the news from across a candlelit table, with Brahm's Lullaby playing softly in the background, evaporated as his caresses grew more insistent. Some things just couldn't be, shouldn't be, planned.

"I think," she said brokenly as his fingers trailed up the sensitive path of her inner thigh, "that you're the one who jumped the gun. About six weeks ago."

The lips pulling gently at her nipple became still as he absorbed her words. His hooded eyes, turbulent with confusion, sought hers.

"You can't be." His voice was barely a whisper, but she heard the hopeful doubt hidden there. "You're on the pill."

She ran a hand along the muscled ridge of his shoulder. "Remember Flagstaff?" she asked, reminding him of the night they'd impulsively decided to spend at a cozy little inn. "Well," she continued, "I'd already just about made up my mind to retire, and then, when you didn't seem worried about my not having my pills, well, I, uh, I guess I got a little lax after that."

The eyes she'd been searching almost fearfully while she made her explanation held her gaze for long, silent moments. Then, incredibly, a sheen of moisture heightened their brightness. His spiky lashes lowered, again hiding his emotions from her, but his hand captured hers and brought it to his lips. The kiss he placed in her cradled palm was as eloquent as the teardrop easing down his masculine cheek.

"I love you," he breathed huskily into her hand, his chest heaving with the weight of his emotions.

"I know," she answered, just before his mouth claimed hers. "I know."

She'd become an expert at reading the signs.

THE EDITOR'S CORNER

1990. A new decade. I suspect that most of us who are involved in romance publishing will remember the 1980s as "the romance decade." During the past ten years we have seen a momentous change as Americans jumped into the romance business and developed the talent and expertise to publish short, contemporary American love stories. Previously the only romances of this type had come from British and Australian authors through the Canadian company, Harlequin Enterprises. That lonely giant, or monopoly, was first challenged in the early 1980s when Dell published Ecstasy romances under Vivien Stephens's direction; by Simon and Schuster, which established Silhouette romances (now owned by Harlequin); and by Berkley/Jove, which supported my brainchild, Second Chance at Love. After getting that line off to a fine start, I came to Bantam.

The times had grown turbulent by the middle of the decade. But an industry had been born. Editors who liked and understood romance had been found and trained. Enormous numbers of writers had been discovered and were flocking to workshops and seminars sponsored by the brand-new Romance Writers of America to acquire or polish their skills.

LOVESWEPT was launched with six romances in May 1983. And I am extremely proud of all the wonderful authors who've been with us through these seven years and who have never left the fold, no matter the inducements to do so. I'm just as proud of the LOVESWEPT staff. There's been very little turnover—Susann Brailey, Nita Taublib, and Elizabeth Barrett have been on board all along; Carrie Feron and Tom Kleh have been here a year and two years, respectively. I'm also delighted by you, our readers, who have so wholeheartedly endorsed every innovation we've dared to make—our authors publishing under their real names and including pictures and autobiographies in their books, and the Fan of the Month feature, which puts the spotlight on a person who represents many of our readers. And of course I thank you for all your kind words about the Editor's Corner.

Now, starting this new decade, we find there wasn't enough growth in the audience for romances and/or there was too much being published, so that most American publishers have left the arena. It is only big Harlequin and little LOVESWEPT. Despite our small size, we are as vigorous and hearty, excited and exuberant now as we were in the beginning. I can't wait to see what the next ten years bring. What LOVESWEPT innova-

(continued)

tions do you imagine I might be summarizing in the Editor's Corner as we head into the new *century*?

But now to turn from musings about the year 2000 to the very real pleasures of next month!

Let Iris Johansen take you on one of her most thrilling, exciting journeys to Sedikhan, read **NOTORIOUS**, LOVESWEPT #378. It didn't matter to Sabin Wyatt that the jury had acquitted gorgeous actress Mallory Thane of his stepbrother's murder. She had become his obsession. He cleverly gets her to Sedikhan and confronts her with a demand that she tell him the truth about her marriage. When she does, he refuses to believe her story. He will believe only what he can feel: primitive, consuming desire for Mallory. . . . Convinced that Mallory returns his passion, Sabin takes her in fiery and unforgettable moments. That's only the beginning of **NOTORIOUS**, which undoubtedly is going onto my list of all-time favorites from Iris. I bet you, too, will label this romance a keeper.

Here comes another of Gail Douglas's fabulous romances about the sisters, *The Dreamweavers*, whose stories never fail to enmesh me and hold me spellbound. In LOVESWEPT #379, **SOPHISTICATED LADY**, we meet the incredible jazz pianist Pete Cochrane. When he looks up from the keyboard into Lisa Sinclair's eyes, he is captivated by the exquisite honey-blonde. He begins to play Ellington's "Sophisticated Lady," and Ann is stunned by the potent appeal of this musical James Bond. These two vagabonds have a rocky road to love that we think you'll relish every step of the way.

What a delight to welcome back Jan Hudson with her LOVESWEPT #380, **ALWAYS FRIDAY**. Full of fun and laced with fire, **ALWAYS FRIDAY** introduces us to handsome executive Daniel Friday and darling Tess Cameron. From the very first, Tess knows that there's no one better to unstarch Dan's collars and teach him to cut loose from his workaholism. Dan fears he can't protect his free-spirited and sexy Tess from disappointment. It's a glorious set of problems these two confront and solve.

Next, in Peggy Webb's **VALLEY OF FIRE**, LOVESWEPT #381, you are going to meet a dangerous man. A very dangerous and exciting man. I'd be surprised if you didn't find Rick McGill, the best private investigator in Tupelo, Mississippi, the stuff that the larger-than-life Sam Spades are made of with a little Valentino thrown in. Martha Ann Riley summons all her courage to dare to play Bacall to Rick's Bogart. She wants to find her sister's gambler husband . . . and turns out to be Rick's

(continued)

perfect companion for a sizzling night in a cave, a wicked romp through Las Vegas. Wildly attracted, Martha Ann thinks Rick is the most irresistible scoundrel she's ever met . . . and the most untrustworthy! Don't miss **VALLEY OF FIRE!** It's fantastic.

Glenna McReynolds gives us her most ambitious and thrilling romance to date in LOVESWEPT #382, **DATELINE: KYDD AND RIOS.** Nobody knew more about getting into trouble than Nikki Kydd, but that talent had made her perfect at finding stories for Josh Rios, the daring photojournalist who'd built his career reporting the battles and betrayals of San Simeon's dictatorship. After three years as partners, when he could resist her no longer, he ordered Nikki back to the States—but in the warm, dark tropical night he couldn't let her go . . . without teaching the green-eyed witch her power as a woman. She'd vanished with the dawn rather than obey Josh's command to leave, but now, a year later, Nikki needs him back . . . to fulfill a desperate bargain.

What a treat you can expect from Fayrene Preston next month—the launch book of her marvelous quartet about the people who live and work in a fabulous house, SwanSea Place. Here in LOVESWEPT #383, *SwanSea Place:* **THE LEGACY,** Caitlin Deverell had been born in SwanSea, the magnificent family home on the wild, windswept coast of Maine, and now she was restoring its splendor to open it as a luxury resort. When Nico DiFrenza asked her to let him stay for a few days, caution demanded she refuse the mysterious visitor's request— but his spellbinding charm made that impossible! So begins a riveting tale full of the unique charm Fayrene can so wonderfully invent for us.

Altogether a spectacular start to the new decade with great LOVESWEPT reading.

Warm good wishes,

Carolyn Nichols

Carolyn Nichols
Editor
LOVESWEPT
Bantam Books
666 Fifth Avenue
New York, NY 10103

FAN OF THE MONTH

Hazel Parker

Twelve years ago my husband Hoke insisted that I quit my job as a data processor to open a paperback bookstore. The reason was that our book bill had become as large as our grocery bill. Today I am still in the book business, in a much larger store, still reading and selling my favorite romance novels.

My most popular authors are of course writing for what I consider to be the number one romance series—LOVESWEPT. One of the all-time favorites is Kay Hooper. Her books appeal to readers because of her sense of humor and unique characters (for instance, Pepper in **PEPPER'S WAY**). And few authors can write better books than Iris Johansen's **THE TRUST-WORTHY REDHEAD** or Fayrene Preston's **FOR THE LOVE OF SAMI.** When the three authors get together (as they did for the Delaney series), you have *dynamite*. Keep up the good work, LOVESWEPT.

60 Minutes to a Better, More Beautiful You!

N ow it's easier than ever to awaken your sensuality, stay slim forever—even make yourself irresistible. With Bantam's bestselling subliminal audio tapes, you're only 60 minutes away from a better, more beautiful you!

__ 45004-2	**Slim Forever**	$8.95
__ 45112-X	**Awaken Your Sensuality**	$7.95
__ 45081-6	**You're Irresistible**	$7.95
__ 45035-2	**Stop Smoking Forever**	$8.95
__ 45130-8	**Develop Your Intuition**	$7.95
__ 45022-0	**Positively Change Your Life**	$8.95
__ 45154-5	**Get What You Want**	$7.95
__ 45041-7	**Stress Free Forever**	$7.95
__ 45106-5	**Get a Good Night's Sleep**	$7.95
__ 45094-8	**Improve Your Concentration**	$7.95
__ 45172-3	**Develop A Perfect Memory**	$8.95

NEW!

Handsome Book Covers Specially Designed To Fit Loveswept Books

Our new French Calf Vinyl book covers come in a set of three great colors—royal blue, scarlet red and kachina green.

Each 7" × 9½" book cover has two deep vertical pockets, a handy sewn-in bookmark, and is soil and scratch resistant.

To order your set, use the form below.

THE DELANEY DYNASTY

Men and women whose loves an passions are so glorious it takes many great romance novels by three bestselling authors to tell their tempestuous stories.

THE SHAMROCK TRINITY

THE DELANEYS OF KILLAROO

THE DELANEYS: *The Untamed Years*

Buy them at your local bookstore or use this page to order.

THE LATEST IN BOOKS
AND AUDIO CASSETTES

Paperbacks —————————————————————

☐	27032	**FIRST BORN** Doris Mortman	$4.95
☐	27283	**BRAZEN VIRTUE** Nora Roberts	$3.95
☐	25891	**THE TWO MRS. GRENVILLES** Dominick Dunne	$4.95
☐	27891	**PEOPLE LIKE US** Dominick Dunne	$4.95
☐	27260	**WILD SWAN** Celeste De Blasis	$4.95
☐	25692	**SWAN'S CHANCE** Celeste De Blasis	$4.50
☐	26543	**ACT OF WILL** Barbara Taylor Bradford	$5.95
☐	27790	**A WOMAN OF SUBSTANCE** Barbara Taylor Bradford	$5.95

Audio —————————————————————————

☐	**THE SHELL SEEKERS** by Rosamunde Pilcher Performance by Lynn Redgrave 180 Mins. Double Cassette	48183-9	$14.95
☐	**THE NAKED HEART** by Jacqueline Briskin Performance by Stockard Channing 180 Mins. Double Cassette	45169-3	$14.95
☐	**COLD SASSY TREE** by Olive Ann Burns Performance by Richard Thomas 180 Mins. Double Cassette	45166-9	$14.95
☐	**PEOPLE LIKE US** by Dominick Dunne Performance by Len Cariou 180 Mins. Double Cassette	45164-2	$14.95

————————————————————————————————